CONTENTS

ACKNOWLEDGEMENTS

All of the stories and sketches within this collection are copyright the Estate of Dorothy Richardson and reprinted with the kind permission of Sheena Odle. With the exception of the stories, 'Summer' and 'Seen from Paradise', which are published here for the first time and copyright 1989, the material included originally appeared in the following periodicals:

'Visitor', *Life and Letters*, 46, pp. 167–72, September 1945; 'Visit', *Life and Letters*, 46, pp. 173–81, September 1945; 'The Garden', *transatlantic review*, 2, pp. 141–43, August 1924; 'Sunday', *Art and Letters*, n.s. 2, pp. 113–15, Summer 1919; 'Christmas Eve', *Art and Letters*, n.s. 3, pp. 32–35, Winter 1920; 'Sleigh Ride', *Outlook*, vol. 58, p. 588 no. 1506, 1926; 'Nook on Parnassus', *Life and Letters Today*, 13, pp. 84–88, December 1935; 'Tryst', W & S Wyatt (eds.), *English Story*, 2nd Series, 1941; 'A Stranger About', *English Story*, 9th Series, pp. 90–94, 1949; 'Ordeal', *Window*, 1 pp. 2–9, October 1930; 'Haven', *Life and Letters Today*, 42, pp. 97–105, August 1944; 'Excursion',

English Story, 6th Series, pp. 107–12, 1945; 'Death', *Weekly Westminster* n.s. 1, 9 February 1924; 'Beginnings', J Gawsworth (ed.), *Ten Contemporaries: Notes Towards Their Definitive Bibliography*, 2nd edition, pp. 195–98, Joiner & Steele, London, 1933; 'A Few Facts for You . . .', *Sylvia Beach*, pp. 127–28, Mercure de France, Paris, 1963; 'What's in a Name?', *Adelphi*, II, pp. 606–9, 7 December 1924; 'Journey to Paradise', *Fortnightly Review*, vol. 123, no. 735, pp. 407–14 March 1928; 'Data for a Spanish Publisher', ed. Joseph Prescott, *London Magazine*, vol. 6, no. 6, pp. 14–19, 1959.

INTRODUCTION

As an elderly woman in 1951, Dorothy Richardson remembered meeting a fortune teller at a garden party some sixty years earlier. The fortune teller foretold that Richardson would marry late and live to an old age and asked if she had done any writing. When Richardson, who was then a young woman under twenty, replied 'No', she was told, simply, 'Begin now'.[1]

It took more than two decades, however, for Richardson to begin to write the first volume of her massive autobiographical novel, *Pilgrimage*. She was then thirty-nine. Despite this late start, her output was considerable, and by the time she died Richardson had produced the thirteen *Pilgrimage* 'chapter-novels' and nearly two hundred shorter pieces – essays, reviews, sketches and short stories. *Pilgrimage* has been republished several times but the shorter writings are scattered throughout little magazines, obscure journals and Richardson's unpublished papers.

This is the first time, then, that Dorothy

Richardson's short works have been presented in book form. *Journey to Paradise* includes all her published stories and autobiographical sketches and two previously unpublished stories. The published stories appeared between 1919 and 1949 and include the last pieces of Richardson's fiction to be printed in her lifetime. Readers of *Pilgrimage* will be interested to see how the author of one of the longest novels in English handles the concise form of the short story. These are curious, enigmatic, pleasurable pieces of writing and will give readers a sense of the strangeness and versatility of Richardson's style. The autobiographical sketches are also rare examples of Richardson's non-fiction accounts of herself. Generally, she was most reluctant to provide biographical material to publishers and journals and for many years very little – not even her date of birth – was known. (Her reluctance on this matter became a form of self parody when, in 1929, she answered the *Little Review*'s request for a photo with a picture of a fat baby.)

In many respects, Richardson's writing is typically modernist in its concern with issues of form and language and its challenge to nineteenth-century assumptions about character, identity and meaning. From its unusual use of sentences and paragraphs to its experiments with size and structure, Richardson's fiction tests the limits of existing literary forms. Her work is notable for its decentred subject, its use of impressionism, its open-endedness and its refusal of fixed meanings. Moreover, it explores the ways in which character and meaning do not precede the literary text but are produced *by* it. Yet Richardson has too often been seen as a pioneer whose work is merely an inferior, female version of the achievements of the modernist men. This judgement fails to do justice to the lively and eccentric qualities of her writing; nor does it recognise the sense of radical otherness one often has in reading her work. Indeed, these aspects of Richardson's fiction have much to offer in a feminist rereading of modernism itself.

Richardson's work is of considerable interest to feminist readers, for her innovative techniques do much to undermine existing assumptions about gender and writing, revealing that acts of representation – stories, novels, films and so forth – involve struggles over meaning which have particular implications for women. In *Pilgrimage* she demonstrates that gender is not fixed or essential, as conceived in much nineteenth-century writing (and indeed in the society of her own time), but is in fact produced and reproduced by a culture and its texts. Her novel questions the oppressive, traditional structures of gender which always place the 'masculine' as superior to the 'feminine', and in doing so, begins to transform them. In her stories and sketches, Richardson deals less obviously with the issue of gender but, importantly, she deals with two related matters: identity and writing. In her work, identity is not something one is born with but is made and remade, through language, throughout one's life. Her characters do not have fixed selves but are 'subjects in process'. And because identity is constructed in language, the act of writing is essential to the creation and understanding of the self. Thus the stylistic innovations of Richardson's work have political implications, for they undermine traditional notions of an essential 'human nature' or 'common sense' which have been used in the past to oppress women.

It is useful in approaching this collection to know some Aspects of her life were quite eccentric and it has been argued that these are connected with her experimental methods of writing.[2] For part of her life though, she was in fact quite typical of a small, almost forgotten, group of women who lived and worked independently in London at the turn of the century. Richardson's friend and fellow writer, Winifred Bryher, was struck by her accounts of the 'actual struggle' women faced between 1890 and 1914, 'when the world for women was a prison, not a universe'. When Bryher first read one of the *Pilgrimage* novels in 1916, she was so delighted to find a feminist description of the world she knew that she immediately telephoned a friend and 'shouted', '*somebody is writing about us*'.[3]

Women like Richardson moved to London to work in badly paid, dull, lower-middle-class jobs. Their reward was a particular kind of freedom: with little leisure time and less money they nonetheless attended lectures, read, engaged in politics and educated themselves. Usually unmarried, sometimes lesbian, financially independent through work – though often on the brink of poverty – these 'New Women' lived in bedsitters and boarding houses and enjoyed a new kind of social freedom. Many wrote novels. Their conditions of life and work are described in detail in parts of *Pilgrimage*, which stands as an important document of women's history of the modernist period.

Many of these women were middle class and had grown up without expecting to work. This was certainly the case for Dorothy Richardson. Her childhood was comparatively wealthy and privileged as her father acquired money from selling the family business. Instead of working, he invested the money – badly, as it turned out – and lived on the proceeds as a 'gentleman', with music and literature and an enthusiastic amateur interest in science. Thus Dorothy Richardson began life in 1873 in an environment of Victorian leisure in Abingdon, Berkshire. (Her early childhood memories form the basis of several of the stories here.) But this comfort and stability steadily declined as her father headed towards bankruptcy. The family was eventually scattered – both geographically and in terms of class – and Richardson was never to be financially secure again.

Because of these financial problems, Richardson decided to leave home at the age of seventeen to work as an English teacher at a girls' school in Germany. This job lasted for only a few months and she returned to England to teach in a school in Finsbury Park, London. She found teaching dull and tiring and in 1895 became a governess. This too was shortlived and she returned, albeit temporarily, to her family. Richardson's father seems to have dominated the family and this, together with their impending bankruptcy, drove her mother into a deep depression which ended in suicide in 1895. Richardson was twenty-two by then and had taken her mother to a hotel in Hastings in the hope that she might recover. After several nights of insomnia and despair, Mary

Richardson cut her throat with a kitchen knife and was found, dead, by her daughter. (These periods of her life are narrated in the first three novels of *Pilgrimage*, published between 1915 and 1917.)

After Mary Richardson's death, the family broke up completely and the following year Dorothy Richardson moved to London to work as a secretary-assistant to a dental surgeon in Harley Street. This marked her final departure from the class of her childhood and it was through this class mobility that she began to realise that the role of 'woman' was not innate or natural, but cultural and subject to change. As she shows through Miriam's experiences in *Pilgrimage*, Richardson found that each new class position she occupied entailed, even at the most trivial level, a new set of conventions for being a woman. As the daughter of a 'gentleman', for example, Richardson was not expected to acquire such domestic skills as cooking or dressmaking (though she did learn some decorative embroidery, as Berry does in the story 'Visitor'). But when she became a middle-class teacher, these attributes were markers of a different notion of 'womanhood' to which she was expected – but unable – to conform. And as a dental secretary she had to learn yet another set of 'feminine' skills to serve her employers and their patients. She was also expected to refrain from speaking out or making demands – which Richardson, like Miriam, seems largely to have failed to do. In *Pilgrimage*, Miriam's gradual discovery of gender as something constructed and changeable is one of Richardson's most radical insights.

For many years, Dorothy Richardson lived in

London on the fringes of Bloomsbury and was involved, erratically, with a wide variety of political groups, including anarchists, suffragists and Fabians. She had a brief affair with H.G. Wells and became pregnant, but miscarried in 1907. This was followed by some kind of nervous breakdown and she left her job to live in the country, where she became very interested in the Quakers. (Later, in 1914, she published two books on the subject: *The Quakers Past and Present* and *Gleanings from the Work of George Fox*.)

It was around this time that she began to write for journals, beginning with some lively reviews and essays for *Ye Crank* (later *The Open Road*), an anarchist journal published by her friends Charles and Florence Daniel. These were followed by some descriptive sketches for the *Saturday Review*, and later she wrote for a variety of other journals, including *The Adelphi*, *Life and Letters*, the *Dental Record* and *Close Up*, a journal of film criticism founded by Bryher. Her journal writings ranged widely, from a column on dentistry and health to book reviews, short stories and feminist essays.

Richardson did not begin to write fiction, however, until 1912, when she went to stay in Cornwall with Jack and Beatrice Beresford. At the end of their holiday, she decided to stay on alone – to write. After several false starts she produced a novel, *Pointed Roofs*, the first book of *Pilgrimage*. (This period in Cornwall is told in the story 'Seen From Paradise', published here for the first time.) It took until 1915 for *Pointed Roofs* to be published, when Edward Garnett – in the first of many such descriptions of Richardson's fiction – described it as 'feminine impressionism' and accepted it for Duckworth.

By this point she was forty-two, and over the next twenty years she produced more 'chapter-novels' of *Pilgrimage* at irregular intervals, until the collected edition – comprising twelve novels, in four volumes and running to more than two thousand pages – appeared in 1938. (A thirteenth novel was added to the posthumous publication of *Pilgrimage* in 1967.) Richardson's first short story was published in 1919, the year in which books four and five of *Pilgrimage* appeared. In all, thirteen stories were published, the last of which came out in 1949, when Richardson was seventy-six. She supplemented the meagre income her fiction generated by working as a proof reader, copy editor, journalist and translator.

In 1917 Dorothy Richardson married Alan Odle, a consumptive artist some fifteen years younger than herself. Despite 'misgivings on both sides', his illness and their continuing poverty, they seem to have had a companionable relationship. They lived in rented rooms in London in the summer and moved to Cornwall most winters for the sake of Odle's health. Though Richardson loved London, she grew to love Cornwall as well, describing it as 'the land of one's adoption'. Alan Odle died there in 1948, aged sixty.

At the height of her career, Dorothy Richardson had a considerable reputation as a modernist novelist. But when she died in a nursing home in 1957, at the age of eighty-four, her reputation had declined so completely that the matron of the home thought her claims to be a writer were senile delusions. It was not until some years after her death that *Pilgrimage* was republished and her shorter writings began to be researched by scholars. With the growth of feminist criticism, Richardson's work has become increasingly well known and respected as an important contribution to literary modernism on the one hand and to feminist fiction on the other.

In her own day, Richardson was widely admired by other feminists and writers. Bryher described her as 'a writer's writer' and Gloria Fromm, her modern biographer, tells of the interest shown in her by other writers when she visited Paris in 1924.[4] She met Hemingway there and he published her story 'The Garden' in the *transatlantic review* when he edited it later that year. A few years later, Ford Madox Ford referred to her as 'that great figure Dorothy Richardson', 'who is still writing, though abominably unknown'.[5] Two of the *Pilgrimage* novels were reviewed at different times by Virginia Woolf, who shrewdly noted 'the discrepancy between what [Richardson] has to say and the form provided by tradition for her to say it in'. She also praised her as a writer who believed 'that the novel is so much alive that it actually grows'. Recognising that Richardson was doing something interesting with literary form and language, Woolf described Richardson's original prose as 'the psychological sentence of the feminine gender'.[6] Other writers, including May Sinclair, Storm Jameson and Rebecca West, paid tribute to her work and John Cowper Powys, a life-long admirer of her writing, wrote a short study of *Pilgrimage* in 1931. (Powys travelled and lectured throughout the United States and he wrote to Richardson that he had met devoted readers of *Pilgrimage* in even the remotest of American towns.) Even today, although Richardson is still 'abominably unknown' to a wide readership, she has a strong following amongst feminist readers and writers. And although she did not always consider herself a feminist, her work is valuable for its complex responses to the gender issues of its time.

Of particular interest are her comments on the relationship between gender and representation. In a 1906 review of an H.G. Wells novel, Richardson is critical of his representation of women for being both static and banal:

> So far he has not achieved the portrayal of a woman . . .
> His women are all one specimen, carried away from
> some biological museum of his student days, dressed up
> in varying trappings, with different shades of hair and
> proportions of freckles, with neatly tabulated instincts
> and one vague smile between them all.[7]

Wells' writing, she suggests, tries to pass off ideologies of gender as if they were 'natural', through his 'biological' notion of women. His portrayal of woman makes her seem wooden, doll-like and mindless: an 'irritating dummy'. A more complex version of this argument occurs in an article entitled 'Women and the Future', published nearly twenty years later. There, she objects to the prevailing idea that there is a 'new species of woman' emerging in the twentieth century. What is really changing, she argues, is not so much women themselves as men's *perceptions* of 'woman', drawn from their representations of her throughout history. This is 'easily understood', Richardson continues, 'when we consider how difficult it is [for both women and men] to *think* the feminine past'. One cannot escape 'the images that throng the mind from the centuries of masculine expressiveness on the eternal theme'; representations of woman which rarely depict her except 'in her moments of relationship to the world as it is known to men'.[8]

Richardson also comments upon the difficulties women face when they wish to participate in art and writing: 'For the woman . . . going into the world of art is immediately surrounded by masculine traditions. Traditions based on assumptions that are largely unconscious and whose power of suggestion is unlimited. Imagine the case reversed', she continues:

> Imagine the traditions that held during a great period of Egyptian art, when women painters were the rule – the nude male serving as model, as the 'artist's model' that in our own day is the synonym for nude femininity.[9]

She concludes with a different, materialist, point about the conditions under which women can work as artists: 'there exists for the woman no equivalent for the devoted wife or mistress'. Moreover, even if a woman *does* have other women to support her:

> the service given by women to women is as different from that given by women to men as is chalk from cheese. If hostile, it will specialize in manufacturing difficulties. If friendly, it will demand unfaltering response. For it knows that living sympathy is there. And in either case service is given on the assumption that the woman at work is in the plot for providing life's daily necessities.

Women, she argues, demand more from each other than they do from men: this idea recurs in _Pilgrimage_, in which Miriam often feels it is other women who force her to conform to a restrictive notion of 'femininity'. Ideological structures cause women to oppress themselves and each other and these are connected, in Richardson's argument, to the participation of women _in_ art and the representation of women _by_ art.

These feminist issues inform both the content and the form of Richardson's fiction. In _Pilgrimage_, they are often confronted overtly, while the stories deal with questions of gender indirectly, mainly through the related issues of identity and writing. Most of the stories and all of the sketches here are autobiographical, and they explore the processes by which a woman learns to perceive herself as _different_ from other people and objects in the world, and the ways in which she can express this.

Like _Pilgrimage_, Richardson's stories show a considerable variation in style, usually related to the maturity and awareness of the protagonist. For this reason, they are arranged here not in order of publication, but roughly according to the age of the main character. Richardson was conscious of writing in a manner appropriate to the development of her characters: _Pilgrimage_ begins in a very simple style – and is often gently ironic about its serious young protagonist – and gradually becomes more complex as Miriam becomes more aware and sophisticated and starts to write herself. The stories do not show quite the same pattern of development, but their linguistic complexity depends upon the age and sophistication of their subject.

Readers of *Pilgrimage* will be particularly interested in the autobiographical sketches, for they offer rare glimpses of her parents and her childhood and retell aspects of Richardson's life which went into the story of Miriam Henderson. Here, too, language is an issue of great importance: the act of naming for example, is mentioned in several of the sketches. In 'What's in a Name?' Richardson writes of the churches she attended as a child and humorously recounts the ways in which a church's name determined its meaning for her. Conversely, in 'Journey to Paradise', she remembers that one of the great joys of her childhood holidays to the seaside was her inability to name the place that she visited. Delighting in the disjunction between words and things, she teases the reader by refusing, still, to name her paradise. (These same holidays are told in fictional form in the story 'Excursion'.)

The title sketch, 'Journey to Paradise', tells of the family holidays in Dawlish in the 1870s. These occurred long before their money ran out and the Richardsons travelled with all the paraphernalia of their class, including special clothes for the journey and servants to assist them. Telling of her childhood memories of the seaside, Richardson compares them with her experiences as an adult, then settles into a long and rather humorous account of the train journey from Abingdon to Devon, which began when 'news of the great journey' came into 'endless summer, into a garden whose boundaries were as yet unknown'. Oddly, it is her environment and not

Richardson herself who receives the news: at this stage of her life she does not have a clear sense of the boundary between herself and the world outside her.

Though 'Journey to Paradise' reads in many ways as a straightforward, if somewhat ironic, piece of autobiographical writing, its meanings are quite difficult to pin down. It is ostensibly an account of her love for her seaside paradise, yet Richardson remarks in passing that what she really loved was not the sea so much as a small stream for which she feels, perversely, 'pity and contempt'. (A similar stream appears in the story 'Tryst'. There, a certain amount of pity and contempt seems to be aimed at the character as well.) And, as the title suggests, Richardson's most important memory is of the journey, not of being there. In fact, paradise is never really achieved, just as *Pilgrimage* does not really arrive anywhere: Richardson's interest is in the processes of an 'eternity' of journeying. Her account of the seaside and of getting there is curiously decentred, giving unexpected weight to things mentioned in passing and undermining the importance of her apparent subject.

A more formal, familiar act of memory occurs in 'Data for a Spanish Publisher'. This curiously titled piece was written rather reluctantly when a Spanish translation of the *Pilgrimage* novels was planned in the 1940s. Under Franco, the Spanish censor banned the books for their 'social subversiveness and atheism'; eventually the ban was lifted but the publication never took place. 'Data' was published posthumously in 1959.

The story of Richardson's life is also summarised in

different forms in 'Beginnings' and 'A Few Facts for You . . .'. In 'Beginnings', she writes mainly of her early childhood in Abingdon and of her memories of first becoming aware of things around her – themes which recur in fictional form in 'Visitor', 'Visit' and 'The Garden'. She also writes of her discovery of 'competition' and 'rivalry' in her early school days and of her recognition of their 'destructiveness'.

'A Few Facts' was published in 1963 in a collection of Sylvia Beach memorabilia and contains a concise summary of Richardson's life. Here she refers to herself in the third person (and as 'D.R.') and portrays herself rather ambiguously as having 'planned a book on the inviolability of feminine solitude or, alternatively, loneliness'. This is quite characteristic of Richardson's uneasy representation of herself, both as a woman in her society and as a feminist. She noted that she rarely read or kept criticism of her work. This was partly because reviewers sometimes mistook her for an American author with the same name, even to the point of the American Richardson's photo being published on several occasions with discussions of the English Richardson's work. This kind of minor confusion over Dorothy Richardson's identity has persisted to the present day and stands as an ironic comment upon the problem of selfhood she explored in her writing. Equally problematic is her historical positioning: she located herself as a pre-World War I novelist and was 'incensed' to find herself 'classified as a post-war writer altogether'. Geographically, London, the seaside, the English countryside and especially Cornwall are the landscapes that were important to her.

*　　*　　*

Richardson's stories tend to be very short and it is interesting to read them against the wordiness of *Pilgrimage*. Often they are rather odd and, like the novel, show a strong resistance to obvious or fixed meanings. As several are autobiographical, they could be seen to extend beyond the time scale of *Pilgrimage*. One often has the sense that Richardson's writing transgresses the boundaries of genre: *Pilgrimage*, for example, refuses to conform to the conventions of either novel or autobiography; it is thirteen separate novels as well as only one and does not seem to be finished. Indeed, it challenges our notions of what 'finished' or 'unfinished' might mean. And in this collection, we find stories which are like autobiographical sketches and autobiographical sketches which read like stories. One piece, 'Sleigh Ride', is at once a descriptive story and an extract from *Oberland* (1927), the ninth novel of *Pilgrimage*. Few of Richardson's stories have the traditional 'sting in the tail'; most are uncertainly ended, opening out, inviting speculation and interpretation. Too often her work is read exclusively in biographical terms: while these are valid, they frequently fail to do justice to the complexity and the challenge to convention posed by her writing.

Some of the stories are strange in an obvious and striking way, such as 'Sunday', her first published story, which tells of a young woman's sense of being oppressed by the obligatory Sunday visit to her deaf grandmother. Anticipation of the visit spoils her day: selfishly, she tries to forget Grannie and her suffering for as long as possible. During the visit, however, she becomes more sympathetic towards the old woman, recognising her physical disabilities and her displacement on to the margins of the family. Then, suddenly, the young woman sees Grannie's room as 'death-soaked', an image setting off a curious series of revelations to which the reader is largely denied access. 'I had thought the thought', says the narrator, 'I had found out how to do it.' But what is 'it'? The narrator feels both liberation and self-loathing as her mind dances across a range of obscured ideas and emotions. It seems that in trying (and largely failing) to communicate with her deaf grandmother, she has suddenly discovered ways to use language as a tool of domination, particularly in its guise of insincere social conversation.

This kind of opaque writing, unrelieved by para-graph breaks, is characteristic of some of the *Pilgrimage* books, notably *Revolving Lights*. It draws attention to itself *as* writing, raises questions about how meaning is produced in narrative and asks what happens when the conventions of narrative are challenged or changed. ('Nook on Parnassus', a story about the simple act of buying some Christmas cards, raises similar difficulties of interpretation. It revolves around the use of snobbery in art, language and social interactions and begins by withholding key pieces of information from the reader.)

Similarly, 'Summer', a previously unpublished account of a young woman travelling in Belgium with her five aunts, avoids easy interpretation. It consists of seven numbered fragments, like brief scenes in a film, with no connecting explanations, and is narrated by the young woman, who – like Miriam in *Pilgrimage* – distances herself from the 'feminine' language and values of the older women. At the beginning of the story, she is aware of her own failure to conform to 'feminine' standards of appearance (the fringe of her hair is straight when it should be curled and her face is shiny with the heat), but she refuses to feel inadequate and boldly leads the aunts in a discussion. 'I was not trying to put anyone right,' she says, 'so the aunts were not offended. That just expresses it, they said, and were grateful and approving, as they would have been with a man.' The young woman places herself in a 'masculine' position here, disdainful of the aunts' 'feminine' view of travelling as 'an affair with strange people looking on all the time, criticising your things'. She refuses to accept the 'feminine' role of putting oneself on display as a spectacle, and treats gender as something which is not innate, but is a position from which one might speak.

This is set in the context of the strangeness of another culture and ends with a funeral seen in the distance which perversely enhances the narrator's sense of the 'happiness and beauty everywhere', in a new place in which values, words and ideas are perceived differently and made strange, through foreign words and unfamiliar customs.

Familiar things are made strange in many of Richardson's stories and in *Pilgrimage* too, as characters learn to see themselves in fresh ways in different places and circumstances. A disabled aunt's visit to the Richardsons in Abingdon forms the basis of 'Visitor'. Throughout the story the external world seems to reflect the actions and feelings of the characters. Parts of the house look different because Aunt Bertha is coming to stay. The child, Berry, cannot discriminate between her own perceptions and the objective world and she is at once sympathetic towards and afraid of the feelings and pain of other beings – at the beginning of the story, she runs away from the canary in his cage to avoid the terrible thought of his loneliness. Then, when Aunt Bertha arrives and has to be helped up the stairs, Berry suddenly wants her – and her suffering – to be whisked from sight. But she soon enjoys the sociability her aunt's visit brings and wants to emulate Bertha's kindness and her 'feminine' passivity in the face of being disabled.

Berry lives in a wealthy family, as the references to the household servants and the long drive leading up to the house indicate. Berry does not understand the significance of these class markers, but she does recognise that Aunt Bertha is different because she lives in 'a cottage thrown into another cottage', has 'chapel hair' and speaks with a Berkshire accent.

Aunt Bertha teaches Berry the traditionally 'feminine' skill of embroidery and helps her to make a religious text for her mother's birthday. Berry admires Aunt Bertha's self-sufficiency as she has a 'party' with her 'materials' and almost wishes she too could be disabled to spend her time in the same way. Her uncertain desire for passive, indoor activity is contrasted with the absent sister Pug's tendency to be 'always somewhere else' – usually outside – 'and grubby'. There is a contradictory sense of longing for freedom on the one hand (which is further explored in 'Visit') and, on the other, for the safe, knowable restrictions that Bertha seems to represent.

But Berry's – and the reader's – sense of *what* Aunt Bertha represents is undermined by the story's ending. Aunt Bertha returns home and the embroidered texts are hung on the wall as presents for Berry's mother. The texts signify their creators – Berry, Pug and Aunt Bertha – and as she looks at them, Berry realises that her aunt is not simply passive or a 'cripple'. It is as though through the embroidered writing Aunt Bertha herself has become a text which can be read: complex, open to interpretation and capable of producing many meanings.

The following story, 'Visit', was originally published with 'Visitor' in *Life and Letters*. The two stories were printed side by side, using the same characters, functioning as if they are two chapters from an unwritten novel and thereby disrupting notions of genre. In 'Visit', Berry and Pug go to stay with Aunt Bertha and some other relations at a Berkshire village, Bilberry Hill. Berry is strongly aware that her relatives are 'chapel' and she wonders why they are not taken to a church and '*shown*'. Shown what? Berry has already absorbed the values of her family and class without understanding them. To her childish self, they are 'common sense' or self-evident truths, but by the end of the story she is dimly aware that other ways of thinking and behaving may be possible.

In both 'Visitor' and 'Visit' we find Richardson's characteristic objectification of people and personification of objects challenging conventional perceptions. As her name suggests, Great-aunt Stone in 'Visit' is perceived by Berry as a frightening, lifeless object, 'sitting in a low armchair with no arms', deaf and blind with 'mauve lips'. 'What is the good of her?' Berry wonders. Like Miriam in *Pilgrimage*, Berry also tends to appropriate the thoughts of others, believing she knows what they feel. Both characters are shown to be mistaken. Other characters have identities and wills separate from the protagonist, a discovery which Berry finds disturbing: she is starting to learn where her society locates its boundaries between self and other.

'The Garden' appeared over twenty years earlier and is an account of Richardson's earliest memory: her 'bee memory', which provides a motif that is repeated in shadowy form in many of the pieces. Here, a very young child spends a few minutes in the family's garden which, for the moment, constitutes her entire world. The language is beautifully simple as the child becomes aware for the first time of objects existing outside herself. But she cannot yet quite distinguish between her own actions and the things around her. Thus, when she walks on the path, it is the gravel which seems to make a noise and the flowers which seem to move. She is surprised to hear the sound of feet when there is 'no one there'. She does not understand that *she* is there, moving, making sounds and having an effect, however slight, upon the world around her.

A strange kind of personification takes place as the child struggles to locate herself and the things in the garden in relation to one another. The parameters between self and other, subject and object are fragile and rather fluid. As she runs away from the garden, she falls and feels pain: not quite in her own body but from the outside – 'the hard gravel holding a pain against her nose'. As she cries and feels a vague sense of injustice, even the crying is separate from herself: 'Coming up out of her body, into her face, hot, twisting it up, lifting it away from the gravel to let out the noise'. The child's experiences in the present are punctuated by glimpses of even earlier memories – of a snowman, of apples ripening – objects from other seasons which the child is learning to recall, but not yet to place.

These three stories are interestingly balanced against Richardson's two stories of old age. In 'Excursion', published in the same year as 'Visitor' and 'Visit', an old woman is on holiday at the seaside with some young people, some of whom (it is not clear which) are her grandchildren. Typically, Richardson omits information one might usually expect in a story and focuses instead on other matters. 'Exursion' begins abruptly, in the middle of something which is not narrated: 'On yet another evening, their voices, gathered together. One voice, in variations.' As the young people talk about various matters in the present, Gran hears a dog's bark which sets off a train of memories of her childhood excursions to the seaside with her family and her sister Pug. All of this is remembered in the first person, but when Gran suddenly returns to the present, the narrative changes and Gran becomes 'she'. The reinforcement of the gap between past and present makes Gran's memories more immediate and vivid to her than her current experiences. The story shifts again between 'I' and 'she' (as *Pilgrimage* does), undermining the reader's sense of quite *who* is narrating.

'Excursion' was published when Richardson was seventy-two and it celebrates old age as a time in which everyone becomes an 'artist': 'No longer seeing experience chronologically', but composing it 'after the manner of a picture, with all the parts in true perspective and relationship'. The 'truth' of perspective and relationship keeps changing, however, with experience constantly remade in memory.

In the last story of the collection, Richardson creates a remarkable portrayal of an old woman dying. Here too the narrative shifts between 'I' and 'she' as the woman thinks of small, practical details in the present – who will milk the cows when she is gone? – and rapidly remembers the large events of her life in the past – marriage, childbirth, widowhood, work. 'Death' describes the sensations of dying from within and without and as the woman finally dies, she returns to a place very much like the garden in the story of the same name, which was published in the same year. (The return to childhood also occurs in 'Ordeal', in which a woman goes into hospital for an unspecified and frightening operation.)

Acts of remembering and retelling aspects of one's life are central to the stories of childhood and old age. Equally important for Richardson is the act of writing, and two of the stories here – 'Haven' and 'Seen from Paradise' – deal specifically with the conditions under which this might be possible. Purling, the main character of 'Haven', has just moved from a noisy boarding house run by 'Mother Shabley' to become a lodger in Miss Tillard's quiet house in the country. He believes he has now found the ideal conditions for writing: solitude, silence and a landlady who is utterly unobtrusive and acquiescent. However, having set up Miss Tillard as an undemanding, invisible version of a wife, Purling is soon dissatisfied with the emptiness of his existence. When he hears Miss Tillard enjoying herself with friends, he realises he has cut himself off completely from human society and resolves to return to the 'lion's mouth' of Mother Shabley's. This story ironically invokes the myth of the writer as lone genius, cut off from the world. More importantly, it examines the assumption that one has to adopt a 'masculine' position in society in order to write. Yet in some ways it endorses this idea in so far as Purling does not expect to spend time doing domestic work.

For Richardson, domestic work was as important and oppressive as paid work, defining the person who performs it and occupying most of her time. She often complained that housework kept her from writing, particularly once she was married, and seems never to have accepted the prevailing idea that women should be forced to accept the unpaid jobs of housework and childcare. Several of her stories explore the 'repellent mystery' of women's domestic responsibilities and analyse the power structures which underlie the distribution of unpaid work. Often Richardson's women characters identify themselves as 'masculine' on this issue and step outside the domestic conspiracy. The women who remain in it are thus doubly marginalised.

As a man, Purling is not required to choose between domestic work and writing. His is the more privileged dilemma of finding the best place to pursue his own interests. 'Haven' was written at a time when Richardson was finding it very difficult to proceed with *Pilgrimage* and it is significant that her only portrayal of a professional writer is also her only portrayal of a man. 'Seen from Paradise' (probably written in 1949) indirectly makes a similar point. In this fictional account of the period Richardson spent in Cornwall in 1912, writing *Pointed Roofs*, the narrator identifies herself with Jim, a man and fellow writer, and one who is exempt from the 'repellent mystery' of housekeeping.

The narrator is curiously ambivalent about her own gender position. She is critical of men for their 'relative helplessness' and their 'dependence, however employed, upon all kinds of service, matters that for them were mysteries without magic', but she also locates herself firmly as one whose work is to write, not to engage in the 'daily palaverings' involved in running a house. Richardson does not discuss the act of writing itself here (though she does in *Pilgrimage*) but rather remembers the events and conditions surrounding her 'first voyage' into fiction. The metaphor of the voyage also occurs in *Pilgrimage*, both in its title (which functions somewhat ironically as a verb – to pilgrimage, to sojourn, to live amongst strangers) and in the metaphor of a journey, undertaken alone, which is used to describe Miriam's sexual encounter with her lover Hypo.[10] Sexuality and writing are often linked in Richardson's fiction and 'Seen from Paradise' slides from the creative voyage to an image of the narrator's ex-lovers and a meditation upon marriage.

'Seen from Paradise' is framed by another piece of writing which signals the end of the narrator's happy solitude. A letter arrives from Jim and Sylvia, announcing their return and requesting that the narrator buy a barrel to serve as a tub for a plant. Her memories of the letter, the plant and the old man who provides the barrels are curiously interwoven throughout the story, creating an impressionistic, non-chronological account of her stay in Cornwall. Once again, there is a strangely decentred quality to this story as no single incident in her memory is given prominence. The result is a most unconventional tale which is as much about the remembering and structuring of events as it is about the events themselves.

There is much to interest and please readers in the pieces in this collection. And although they are politically and formally less radical than *Pilgrimage*, they are nonetheless a good introduction to the eccentricities of Richardson's feminism. Her readership is gradually expanding: studies of her life and work have begun to appear regularly in the last decade and two volumes of her letters are currently in preparation. Increasingly, Dorothy Richardson is being recognised for her contribution to the feminist literature of modernism: a 'dangerous critic sitting unnoticed in the corner'[11] of an eminent domain no longer populated exclusively by men.

Trudi Tate, Cambridge, 1988

NOTES

1 'Seven Letters from Dorothy M. Richardson', (ed.) Joseph Prescott, *Yale University Library Gazette*, 33, p. 107, 1959.
2 Gillian Hanscombe, *The Art of Life: Dorothy Richardson and the Development of Feminist Consciousness*, Peter

Owen, London, 1982; Gillian Hanscombe and Virginia
Smyers, *Writing for their Lives: The Modernist Women
1910-1940*, The Women's Press, London, 1987.

3　Bryher, *The Heart to Artemis: A Writer's Memoirs*,
Collins, London, 1963; 'D.R.', *Adam International
Review*, 31, p. 22, 1967.

4　Gloria Glikin Fromm, *Dorothy Richardson: A Biography*,
pp. 165-66, University of Illinois Press, Urbana, 1977.

5　Ford Madox Ford, *The March of Literature: From
Confucius to Modern Times*, pp. 755, 773, George Allen
and Unwin, London, 1947.

6　Virginia Woolf, 'The Tunnel', *Times Literary Supple-
ment*, p. 81, 13 Feb 1919; 'Romance and the Heart',
Nation and Athenaeum, p. 229, 19 May 1923, rpt. in
Women and Writing, ed. Michèle Barrett, pp. 188-92,
The Women's Press, London, 1979.

7　'In the Days of the Comet', *Ye Crank*, 4, p. 376, Novem-
ber 1906.

8　'Women and the Future', *Vanity Fair*, 22, pp. 39–40,
April 1924.

9　'Women in the Arts', *Vanity Fair*, 24, p. 100, May 1925.

10　*Pilgrimage* 4, p. 257, Virago Press, London, 1979.

11　'Novels of the Week: Dorothy Richardson', *Times Literary Supplement*, p. 799, 17 Dec 1938.

FURTHER READING

Barrett, Michèle and Jean Radford, 'Modernism in
the 1930s: Dorothy Richardson and Virginia Woolf',
in Francis Barker *et al.*, eds., *The Sociology of Literature, I: The Politics of Modernism*, pp. 252-72, University of Essex, Colchester, 1979.

Rachel Blau DuPlessis, *Writing Beyond the Ending:
Narrative Strategies of Twentieth Century Women*

Writers, Indiana University Press, Bloomington, 1985.

Mary Ellmann, *Thinking about Women*, Macmillan, 1968; rpt. Virago Press, London, 1979.

Avrom Fleishman, *Figures of Autobiography: The Language of Self-Writing in Victorian and Modern England*, University of California Press, Berkeley, 1983.

Gloria Glikin Fromm, 'What are Men to Dorothy Richardson?' in Janet Todd, ed., *Women and Literature*, vol. 2, pp. 168-88, Holmes and Meier Publishers, New York and London, 1981.

Diane Filby Gillespie, 'Political Aesthetics: Virginia Woolf and Dorothy Richardson', in Jane Marcus, ed., *Virginia Woolf: A Feminist Slant*, pp. 132-51, University of Nebraska Press, Lincoln and London, 1983.

Stephen Heath, 'Writing for Silence: Dorothy Richardson and the Novel', in Susanne Kappeler and Norman Bryson, eds., *Teaching the Text*, pp. 126-47, Routledge and Kegan Paul, London, 1983.

Sydney Janet Kaplan, *Feminine Consciousness in the Modern British Novel*, University of Illinois Press, Urbana, 1975.

Esther K. Labovitz, *The Myth of the Heroine: The Female Bildungsroman in the Twentieth Century: Dorothy Richardson, Simone de Beauvoir, Doris Lessing, Christa Wolf*, P. Lang, New York, 1986.

Jane Miller, *Women Writing About Men*, Virago Press, London, 1986.

John Rosenberg, *Dorothy Richardson, the Genius they Forgot: A Critical Biography*, Duckworth, London, 1973.

SHORT STORIES

VISITOR

BECAUSE Aunt Bertha is coming, something has come into the room. Making it different. The others must be thinking of her, too, but they don't seem to notice that the room is different. Too full, although Pug is not here. She is somewhere else, getting grubby, not thinking about Aunt Bertha.

Mother and Mary and Ellen are standing up and talking. They are going. They will take it with them. Yes, It is going away. There will be plenty of room for it out in the hall. Berry follows them into the passage leading to the hall, sees, through the open garden door, the slack tennis-net waiting, alone. Running along into the hall, she sees them all standing talking at the wide-open front door. It is out in the garden now: sending in a broad blaze of sunlight. Not here in the drawing-room which is *always* waiting for people to come. Berry runs down its length and out into the conservatory. The plants and ferns don't notice her. Perhaps Aunt Bertha isn't coming after all.

Loud voices in the hall, sending away the lovely smell from her fingers that had just pinched a leaf of

2

scented geranium. Aunt Bertha has come. Running
out through the conservatory door she sees the back
garden smiling to itself, looking like tomorrow. Down
the steps and up the other steps and in by the back
door and into the breakfast-room, to be back for a
minute in the waiting for Aunt Bertha to come.

'*Sweet!*'

Dickie, in his cage, all alone. 'Sweet little Dick!'
Berry runs away, to forget the pain of Dickie's loneliness, to lose the worse pain, just coming, of the
thought of his nights alone under his baize cover.

The letter-cage half of the front door is bolted back
as well as the other. They are all out in the porch and
Berry can hear wheels creaking and scrunching on
the drive. Ann bounces quickly into the hall from the
back stairs, setting her cap straight. And now they
are all on the steps below the porch, hiding Aunt
Bertha. But Berry can imagine what Aunt Bertha has
seen as she came up the drive between the high trees:
the bed of shrubs in bloom in the middle of the sweep,
lobelias thick all round the edge – did Aunt Bertha
notice how *blue* they are? – the green lawn with the
stone vases at the corners filled with calceolarias, so
bright in the sun.

'Eh, Bertha, well, me-*dear*.' Mother's voice like
when you are ill, forgetting the garden and telling
Aunt Bertha she is a cripple. Berry goes down the
steps and gives Ellen a little push to get between her
and Pug and see what Aunt Bertha is like. Perhaps
she will stop being a cripple.

Short arms stuck out, jerking from side to side.
Aunt Bertha on a visit, working herself forward on
the seat of a bathchair, not looking at anybody,

staring in front of her with her mouth open and her chin jutted out; feeling pain. Ann and the bath-chairman one on each side, not able to help because of the jerking arms. Presently she will be inside the house.

Berry wants them to push her back into the chair and trundle her away.

'Now then!' cries Aunt Bertha. She has sent up her underlip outside the other and is pressing so hard that it makes two lines, pains, one each side of her mouth. Ann and the chairman crook their arms under hers and she comes up bent forward, sticking out behind, with the hem of her dust-cloak sticking out still further. Her bent-over head comes round. A bull-ock in a straw hat. It does not move. But her eyes are moving. She looks at everybody in turn and smiles, and leaves off looking like a bullock.

Berry runs away, runs upstairs into the empty school-room that knows nothing about Aunt Bertha. But Berry knows. She looks at the lines turning into a smile, and looks into the brown eyes that know what was there when they were all waiting for her to come.

When Berry comes into the dining-room Aunt Bertha is sitting at the table with the others. Lunch is roast fowl, and wine-glasses. Aunt Bertha looks like a visi-tor, making a party. Someone has brought Dickie in. He is singing without stopping to breathe. So happy. No need to speak when she goes round to shake hands with Aunt Bertha, because everybody is talking louder than usual until Dickie stops.

When Aunt Bertha says anything she does not look

at anybody. Her eyelids go down and the pains in her freckled white face look sharper while she thinks of what she is saying and all the same she goes on managing the things on her plate, carefully, while she is talking and you don't know who she is going to look at until the end of what she says, and then she looks suddenly at whoever it is; and smiles.

Aunt Bertha is chapel. She has chapel hair, parted and shined back into a little ball behind her head. But muslin tuckers, fresh and new, round her white neck where there are no freckles, and coming out from under the brown silk dress sleeves on to her hands, gently.

Berry is grown-up. Sitting in a brown silk? with Sunday frills, managing a peach like that: letting it sit for a while in the middle of the plate being a lovely ripe peach; forgetting it and sitting up very straight, with her head turned to say something to someone quite at the other end of the table, but knowing all the time that the peach is there and presently taking up the silver knife and fork, very gently, so that they have time to shine as they move, and then doing the peeling and slicing in and out of what she is saying until at last she is saying something with the first little piece of peach standing still on the end of the fork, while she finishes what she is saying, and smiles. And then pops the piece of peach into her mouth and goes far away while someone else says something.

But Berry does not want to say bro-ther, in two words. Or live in a cottage thrown into another cottage, and make eight-een dressed dawls for a bazaar to buy a new chapel harmonium.

*   *   *

Berry sits at work, bent over it like Aunt Bertha, with a very quiet, calm face. Perhaps after a while, if she can go on feeling like this after Aunt Bertha has gone away, she will learn always to be pale and quiet and suddenly smile all over her face when she speaks. And learn to say something that is true, but not easy to say, so funnily that no one will mind. My *work*, Aunt Bertha says, and, your *work*. Important. Fancywork. No. I Know that my Redeemer Liveth cannot possibly be fancy-work.

She thinks of the patchwork she will be doing when Miss Webb comes back. Miss Webb calls it learning to sew. And at first it was trying to keep the cotton clean and make neat stitches without a row of little blood-dots. And now it is easy. But Miss Webb does not know anything about the look of the different little pieces out of the rag-bag in the wardrobe-room, all smelling of lavender. She does not see the far-away inside of the little lilac pieces with the small pattern, nor want to look and look into the pattern and find out why it goes so deep. She does not know that the striped pieces are horrid.

Aunt Bertha looks up. But only so far as the bunch of skeins. Her eyes see the skeins, but she is thinking about something else. Her thoughts go on while she takes a fresh thread without ever looking across. With the point of her needle she presses back a little piece of fray and makes the next stitch so that it will just hold it down. Berry wishes there were a piece of fray in her text. But there is only to see that the thick gold silk goes into the right holes. And now Aunt Bertha is sitting back with her head on one side and her eyes screwed up to see how her work looks from a distance. And now she is going on with it, looking very stern. Lifting her head, Berry holds it on one side and screws up her eyes and sees all she has done, without looking from letter to letter: I know that my Re, looking so lovely that she cannot believe she has made it, and almost wishes she were a cripple so as to sit all day, like Aunt Bertha, having a party with her 'materials'. Different coloured silks and many needles and a little silver thimble and ornamental scissors and presently something finished and looking lovely. And then thinking of something else to make.

The text is more than half finished, not counting the diamond-shaped full stop at the end. Her hand goes out to pat the worked silk, but quickly comes back as she remembers: Don't handle the silks but when you're threading them. The smooth gold bands of the letters are as clean as the silk in the skeins; and brighter. Much nicer than Pug's. Pug's text is in smaller letters: God is Love. Short, like Pug. And Aunt Bertha has done most of it because Pug is nearly always somewhere else and grubby. And there are only three days before Mother's birthday. Aunt Bertha will be gone; not sitting in the breakfast-room, making it like a party all the morning; not going for drives with Mother and coming back and making tea-time like a party. She will be at home in the cottage thrown into another cottage.

Secretly, in Mother's bedroom, Mary takes the texts out of the parcel. Pug's is on the top. Small. It comes out of its wrapper and there it is, a framed picture held up by Mary. Ellen says isn't it lovely and it is lovely, lovely; the crimson letters in the chestnut-brown frame. Ellen takes down Mother's smallest picture and they hang up Pug's text, to try. Pug, hanging up on the wall for everyone to see. And now Mary's hands are on the paper covering the other text. Frightened, Berry feels. Shuts her eyes. Cannot move or speak. Sees, in her shut eyes, the big beautiful Redeemer in glossy, golden letters, and the rest not finished. But she can *remember* finishing it, and doing the diamond shape and the difficult scroll. She opens her eyes. Mary is taking off the wrapping. Away, away out on to the landing.

'Lovely,' Mary's voice. Berry runs to the other end of the landing, with the word ringing in her ears. Outside the end window she sees the climbing roses looking in at her.

'Berry!'

Where to hide? In the housemaid's cupboard, crouched, hearing her breathing tell Ann's brooms she is there, hearing Mary and Ellen go downstairs. Out of the cupboard, quickly across the landing, to look. There it is. Over the mantelpiece, the lovely golden words and the full stop and the scroll, hanging crooked. And too high to reach. And Mother will be coming up, sent up, Mary said, alone, 'on some excuse' to find the birthday surprise.

'There, darling. It's quite straight now, my chick. It's a beautiful text, and you've done it very nicely, bunny-chub. Mother likes it very much indeed.'

'The full stop is diamond-shape.'

'Yes, my darling.'

'Not round, like an ordinary full stop.'

'No, dearie, it's a beautiful full stop.'

Mother goes on looking at the text and Berry comes quite near; to see her face while she is looking. It is sad, and a hairpin she doesn't know about is sticking out, ready to fall.

'Poor Bertha!'

Berry feels a thump in her heart, and her face grows hot: stupid, stupid Mother. She only knows Aunt Bertha is a cripple. Why can't she see her, up there, in the text, on the wall? She is spoiling the text, because she can't *see*.

VISIT

T HE carriage door is shut. The guard shows all his teeth again, touches his cap to Mary, blows his whistle and goes away to get into the train. The train gives a jolt and the platform, with Mary on it waving her hand, moves away until all the station has gone and there are fields. This is the Journey. There is Pug, opposite. But not like she is at home. Like a stranger. Berry feels alone.

The wheels keep saying: Going-to, going-to, Bilberry Hill, Bilberry Hill, Bilberry HILL. If they went more slowly, they would be saying something else. But they hurry because they know they must get to Bilberry Hill. All the time it is coming nearer. Not like it was in the garden, when Mother said about going, and Berry and Pug had danced round the lawn singing Off to Philadelphy. Berry looks across at Pug and sees that she knows it is not the same.

When another station has come, the guard looks in at the window with his teeth and goes away, waving his flag. The wheels begin again, slowly. Auntbertha, they say, Unclehenry, Unclealbert, Greatauntstone.

Another station and the guard comes and says: 'Next station, young ladies!' and Berry thanks him politely and looks at Pug as soon as he is gone, to try and feel happy. But Pug's face says there is no help. Home is gone, for three whole days. Berry stares at Pug, trying to think of something to make her say something instead of just sitting there with her pug-face, nose all screwed up, like looking out of the window when it rains on a holiday.

'Watery-boughtery-*ceive*,' says Pug, and looks away, trying to show she does not care. But she does care. She is thinking of the strange place and strangers.

'Great-aunt Stone won't say grace for *tea*,' says Berry, and feels better. Busy, with things to explain to Pug. Pug is wondering about blind Great-aunt Stone. She has never seen a private blind person. 'Pug, if you think Great-aunt Stone will be wearing a cardboard label, she won't.'

It is a little station, with wet bushes. Nobody there. The guard comes and lifts them out into a smell of sweetbriar.

'There's yer uncle, that's Mr Albert. getting out of the chaise.'

Berry stands looking. Her feet won't move. A countryman is coming in at the little gate, looking about, jerking his head, with his eyes nearly shut because the sun is in them. He comes across the platform, to take them to Uncle Albert.

'Ber-rie an' Nan-cie?'

It can't be Uncle Albert. But it is Uncle Albert. His mouth is pulled sideways to pretend he is not frightened. But he is frightened.

'I'll drive y'long.' He turns round and waits a seconds as if he is not sure Berry and Pug will follow, and then goes on, in a jerky walk, showing off, all to himself.

The chaise is very low, almost on the ground, so that the dusty, fat pony looks too large. When they are inside with the little portmanteau standing on end, they all seem too large and close together. Close together, and all alone. Uncle Albert has to sit sideways to drive. All the time, every day, he is frightened, ashamed, like a little boy in disgrace. But now he is being very grand because there is nobody there.

'Chee-er up!'

He has seen we think him dreadful and are not liking the bumpy drive in the little basket.

'I'm sure,' Berry says, and hears her voice come out frightfully loud: 'we shall be very happy.'

'Chee-er up, Carrie!' says Uncle Albert, flicking the pony with his whip. He is not thinking about us at all. Berry sits quite still, with the blush burning her face, and looks at the shining back of the pony where the big bones move under the fat. They are going downhill and the chaise shakes and bumps, and a polite cough Pug gives comes out in two pieces.

'How's all at home?'

'Quite-well-thank-you.' Pug has not said anything yet. But she is sitting up nicely and her face is looking polite. A village has come. Uncle Albert stops at a butcher-shop.

'Got that for me, Mr Pi-ther?' he shouts in a high, squeaky voice.

Pug is pinching Berry's arm and looking up the street. 'Look!' she says in a loud whisper: 'Bald-faced

Stag!' Berry pretends not to hear. 'Berry! Bald –' 'Sh'
says Berry and feels like Miss Webb. Pug is quiet at
once. She knows it is rude to make remarks. And she
is silly to expect a village public house to be called
The Northumberland Arms. There is honeysuckle
somewhere. But Pug doesn't smell it because she is
still looking out for something funny.

Mr Pither comes out of his shop in a large white
apron, with a parcel, and looks. He has no whites to
his eyes; like a horse.

'Nice after the sha-oo-er. So ye found the little
misses.' He smiles into the chaise with his eyelids
down as he puts in the parcel. Berry watches the
eyelids to say good afternoon when they come up.
Uncle Albert says thankee Mr Pi-ther and gives a
click and the pony moves and Mr Pither looks down
the street. He is thinking about the village, the only
place he knows.

A cottage, hidden in dark creepers, joined on to
another cottage, plain white. As Berry goes up the
little path, the strange cottage seems to be one she
has been into before. She knows she has never been
into it, and yet feels her face suddenly get unhappy
because she must go again into a place she doesn't
like.

'Come in, children!'

Aunt Bertha's voice, in a room. It is low and small
and musty, sending away the summer. Aunt Bertha is
there, twisted round in her chair, to welcome. While
Berry kisses her she sees home and the mornings with
Aunt Bertha, making the Text, and Aunt Bertha smiles
and sees them, too, but after Pug has quickly kissed her

she only says now go and give your Great-auntie a kiss,
and the little room is full of Great-aunt Stone sitting in a
low armchair with no arms. The back of it, going up
beyond her head, looks like half a pipe.

Aunt Stone does not move or speak as Berry goes
towards her. Her eyes are open, staring at nothing,
with a film over them like the fish on the slab at Pratt's.

'Mother! Berry!'

So Great-aunt Stone is deaf as well as blind. What is
the good of her, sitting there? That is what happens if
you are eighty-five. You sit somewhere being no good.

'How do you do, Aunt Stone?' Berry asks, speaking
very loud, to be heard. And now Aunt Stone knows she
is there, because the dreadful mauve lips are going to
speak and one of the twisted hands, with the big mauve
veins standing up on it, comes a little way off her knee.

'Give me a kiss, my-little-dear.'

When her own face is near enough to the dreadful
old face she must kiss, Berry shuts her eyes. But just
before her eyelids go down she sees a piece of sunlight
on the wall behind the chair and stays in it while she
gives her kiss and thinks of how she will be able to look
at it again presently; but remembers politeness:

'This is my sister Nancy,' she shouts, and bumps into
Pug standing too near behind.

It is rude to be seeing Aunt Bertha frowning and being
cross. Every day, for every meal, someone has to get
her to the table like this. Perhaps Uncle Albert always
makes the same mistakes, making her angry. At home
she clung on to the servants' arms and made little jokes
as she came, and made funny faces at Pug and me to
make us laugh. Aunt Bertha on a visit happy and

polite. This is Aunt Bertha at home. Quite different.
Angry like a little girl, and making Uncle Albert frightened. She knows I have seen, and is smiling at me now
that she is sitting down; and I can't smile back.

Those things she can see on the other side of the
room as she sits at the tea-table beside Pug have
always been there, making a home like other things
make other homes; a grandfather clock with a private
face, high up above everybody; plush frames on the
walls with bunches of flowers inside, painted by
hand; a sheffa-near with a mirror and photographs in
plush frames and a bowl, like the bowl of dried rose
leaves at home: po-pooery. I am on a visit to all of
them, and not to the uncles and aunts. They are
always there, whatever happens. And the little patch
of sunlight is often there, like someone saying something special.

There is no bread-and-butter. The *loaf* is on the
table and a dish with a large round of butter with a
picture of a cow on the top, and a little china beehive.
No cake. A dish with a Yorkshire pudding in it. But
jam, and a bowl of cream. Uncle Albert is cutting
bread-and-butter, screwing up his face and being
almost as grand as he was in the chaise. Aunt Bertha
is looking at him, frowning. Suddenly she tells Berry
to begin. As if she has been seeing her without looking, and knows she has not begun. And now she and
Pug are eating lovely new crusty bread-and-butter.
Bilberry Hill. It goes down being Bilberry Hill, not
tasting of the musty smell in the room. Berry looks at
the lovely little beehive, munching and thinking how
unkind it is to be happy without caring about the
aunts and Uncle Albert although it is their bread-and-

butter and their beehive. Perhaps they are happy,
too? She looks at Aunt Bertha, and Aunt Bertha is
smiling at her like she used to do at home. And now
she is leaning over and helping Berry to honey out of
the beehive.

'Would Berry like a piece of lardy-cake?'

Berry quickly says yes please and looks all round
the table again, for cake. But there is not any cake.
Uncle Albert is cutting out a corner of the Yorkshire
pudding, and now he has slid it on to her plate. When
she has taken a small bite, she wants to talk about it.
It is like the outside of very brown doughnuts, only
much nicer and crisp. Uncle Albert is looking at her
with his head on one side and is going to speak. She
wishes he wouldn't, wishes nobody would look or
speak to her. The cake won't go on tasting so good if
she must think of people too.

'Ye won't get that,' Uncle Albert's voice is angry, as if
I had done something wrong – 'not outside Burksheer.'

'Did ye get that bitta brisket, Albert?'

Now they are all attending to Aunt Stone and something they all know about. I am alone with the lardy-
cake and Pug. She is eating her piece neatly, in nice
little bites, but listening too.

Suddenly Pug's voice comes out: 'We have all our
meat done in a roasting-jack in front of the fire.'

'That'll be Jo-erge,' says Uncle Albert.

'And Father cuts the usparrygus; not gardener.'

Berry kicks hard, sideways, and hits Pug's ankle
and Pug stops and Berry quickly sighs and says I'm
awfully happy, to make up for Pug showing off, and as
soon as she has said this without meaning it, she
means it, and wants to be staying at Bilberry Hill for a

long time, long enough to see everything there is,
instead of just three days.

Eliza picks up the candle and says goodnight little
misses and opens the door. She doesn't want to stay
and she doesn't want to go. Her footsteps creak, like
her voice. They are the only footsteps and voice she
has. She will have them when she is back in the kitchen.

Black darkness. Taking away the walls. You can
only tell it is the same room by the musty smell. All the
things are in it like they were when the candle was
there. The Chair. No, no, NO! I *won't* see the Chair.

'Pug,' very quietly, just to show she is there, even if
she is asleep. She is asleep. Berry pokes her eyelids,
to make colours. Where do they come from, these
pretty colours? When the colours are gone, the Chair
is there, inside her eyes, with Great-uncle Stone sitting in it. Dead. Like Eliza said they found him. But
with certainly a gold watch-chain. Look at the watch-
chain. All gold and shining, like it was when he was
going about the house and going out. Going to Wesleen
chapel. But one day he couldn't go out. He came
upstairs and sat in that Chair. For ten years.

'Pug!'

Pug is asleep, far away. Berry turns quickly round,
to be nearer to her. The quilt crackles as she turns,
telling her to remember the pink roses on it. They are
still there, in the dark. And it isn't quite, quite dark.
Over there, in the corner, is a little square of faint
light showing through the window curtain, telling
about getting up in the morning, with Pug.

Rose leaves and roses, coming in at the window,

almost touching the little washstand. Berry washes very slowly, to be staying as long as possible, with her back to the room, in this corner where the morning comes in with the roses. Not talking to Pug. Just being altogether Berry.

Downstairs, it is dark. In the Morning. Uncle Henry is still not there. Uncle Albert has a shiny face and a Cambridge blue tie; for Sunday. But he cuts large slices of the cold bacon, and it is lovely; very mild and with pink fading away into the fat part.

After breakfast Uncle Henry suddenly comes in. He has a black beard, but all the same is short like Uncle Albert. He says some of the things relations say, only in the funny way they all speak at Bilberry Hill. Then he goes away behind his beard and is sad. And frightened too. But not of people, like Uncle Albert.

It is nice running down the lane with Uncle Henry, joining hands and running and laughing, out in the sunlight. When he laughs, his white teeth come out of his black beard. But the lane ends in a muddy yard, with pigs running about and grunting. Pug says aren't they funny. But they are not funny. They are dirty and frightened.

'Race you back,' says Uncle Henry, and runs up the lane very fast and into the house. And now there is only the sitting-room again, and Uncle Henry gone away somewhere. There's nothing to do but look through the glass of the door that goes into the garden; until Aunt Bertha comes down to read Line upon Line. Perhaps she can find the piece about a bell and a pomegranate, a bell and a pomegranate, round about the hem of Aaron's robe.

Aunt Bertha said not to play in the garden until tomorrow. But we can just open the door and look.

There is a little pavement outside, running along the back of the cottage.

'Come along, Pug. This isn't the garden.'

The little path is very nice. Secret. Pug is just behind me, liking it too. Only somewhere in front, further along there is a dreadful harmonium sound; wheezy and out of tune. The path reaches the plain white part of the cottage, and the slow, dismal sound is quite near. Just inside this door. Another sitting-room. Perhaps that is where Uncle Henry went. Berry opens the door: Uncle Albert. All alone, sitting at a crooked harmonium, playing How Sweet the Name in a bare room with no carpet, and bulging sacks lying about on the floor. Poor Uncle Albert playing, all out of tune and out of time, the only Sunday music he knows. Holding on to it; all alone.

Quickly Berry closes the door, pushes past Pug, runs back along the little path. Half-way along, she is back again at the creeper-covered cottage. Where to go? Where is Sunday? Why don't chapel people stop being chapel? Why aren't they taken to church, and shown? But Sunday must be here; somewhere. Perhaps at the far end of the path, near that tree.

'Is 'Enery back?' Great-aunt Stone's voice, shaky, calling from her room upstairs. 'Tellim I wantim to cut my toe-nails.'

'Come on, Pug, come in!' Somewhere inside is Uncle Henry and his beard, being looked for. He is Aunt Stone's favourite and must do this dreadful thing for her. Perhaps this afternoon he'll take us out somewhere. Away. Tomorrow we can go in the garden. The next day we shall be at home. But all the things here will be the same when we're not seeing them.

*　　*　　*

Not a real garden. No lawn. Nowhere to play.
Nowhere to forget yesterday in. Only this one little
path going along between the vegetables and goose-
berry bushes to the end: trees, and thick shrubs and a
wall. And Pug coming along the path not very happy,
waiting for something nice and already seeing there's
nothing.

It is a wooden door, right in the middle of the wall;
nearly covered with creepers.

'Pug!' Pug comes running; is near. Good little Pug,
not saying anything, waiting to be told what to do. I
can smell the lineny smell of her pinafore. The gate
won't move. It *won't*.

'Hold on to me, and pull!'

Wudge. It's open.

A green hill, going up into the sky. A little path at
the bottom for people to walk and go somewhere.

'Pug. *Pug*!'

Berry runs up the bright green grass. Into nowhere.
Sees the wind moving the grass. Feels it in her hair.
No one knows about this hill. No one knows it is there.
Near the top she stands still, to remember how it
looked from the door; long, long ago. It will always
look like that. Always. Always. She lies down, to smell
the grass, puts her cheek against it, feels grass blades
in her ear.

'Pug! This is the country. Bilberry Hill. We've found
it.'

Pug looks down at her, standing still, waiting. Berry
hides her face in the grass, to be alone.

'Berry! Aren't you glad we are going home
tomorrow?'

'I don't know.'

THE GARDEN

THERE was no one there. The sound of feet and no one there. The gravel stopped making its noise when she stood still. When the last foot came down all the flowers stood still.

Pretty *pretty* flowers. Standing quite still, going on being how they were when no one was there. No one knew how they were when they stood still. They had never seen them like this, standing quiet all together in this little piece.

They were here all the time, happy and good when no one was here. They knew she was happy and good. Feeling shy because they knew it. They all put their arms round her without touching her. Quickly. And went back, sitting in the sun for her to look at.

She could see the different smells going up into the sunshine. The sunshine smelt of the flowers.

The bees had not noticed her. They were too busy. Zmm. Talking about the different colours coming out at the tops of the stalks. Keeping on making dark places in the air as they crossed the path. Some standing on their hind legs just as they were choosing which flower.

Some of the flowers seemed not so nice. As she looked at them they quickly said they loved her and were nice.

A little flower looking out from several all alike. Being different. A deep Sunday colour. Too deep. The sun did not like it so much. The sun liked the blue and pink best. This piece of garden was the blue and pink and all their many leaves. Poor leaves. Perhaps they wanted to be flowers . . .

Wherever she looked she could see this one different flower, growing taller. It was Nelly on a stalk. She went nearer to see if it would move away. It stood still, very tall. Its stalk was thin. She put her face down towards it to keep it down. It had a deep smell. She touched it with her nose to smell more. It kissed her gently, looking small. A tiny plate, cut into points all round the edge. Perhaps now it would go away.

'Dear little flower.'

It knew all about the other part of the garden. The bent-over body of Minter. The little thrown marrow had hit him. He had not minded. Old Minter alone with the Ghost.

The smell of the dark pointed trees in the shrubbery. Raindrops outside the window falling down in front of the dark pointed trees. The snowman alone on the lawn, after tea, with a sad slanted face.

Shiny apples on the trees on Sunday with pink on one side.

The slippery swing seat, scrubby ropes, tight. Tummy falling out, coming back again high in the air . . .

The apples were near this part. In the sun. Where the cowslip balls hung in a row on the string.

It was safe out here with the flowers. Nothing could come here, on the path between the two sides coming down at their edges in little blues sitting along the path with small patted leaves. All making a sound. They liked to bulge out over the warm yellow gravel, like a mess.

Far away down the path where it was different It could come. It could not get here. The flowers kept it away. It was always in other parts of the garden. Between the rows of peas. Always sounding in the empty part at the end.

Outside the garden it was dark and cold. Spring-heeled Jack jumped suddenly over the hedges. The old woman with the basket, watching up the drive. Perhaps the flowers would always keep them away now.

Perhaps if she went back now the flowers would follow her. She turned right round and ran. They did not come. Panting came at once. The big path by the lawn ached with going so fast. In front were the pointed trees sitting on the piece of lawn that came out and made the path narrow. Just round the corner, soon, just past the bit of the house that had no window, was the stable and the back porch. Coming. There they were. There were a few little flowers by the back porch, cook's flowers, not able to get away into the garden. Not able to go inside the kitchen. They were always frightened. They made the panting worse.

Bang. The hard gravel holding a pain against her nose. Someone calling. She lay still hoping her nose would be bleeding to make them sorry. Here was crying again. Coming up out of her body, into her face, hot, twisting it up, lifting it away from the gravel to let out the noise. Someone would come, not knowing about the flowers; the pretty, pretty flowers. The flowers were unkind, staying too far off to tell them how happy and good she was.

SUNDAY

I

I LOOKED up and saw Josephine cutting cake.
Until that moment every moment of Sunday had
been perfect. The day had been so perfect that I had
forgotten there was anything in the world but its
moments and they were going on for ever, and I was
just turning blissfully towards the walk across the
common; daylight still on the greenery, and the
Hopkins in *F* service with candles burning in twilight
and the frivolous evening congregation. I looked
drunkenly up to look down the envious room at my
green soul holding the window clean open from outside and pouring in and holding them all in affection-
ate envious silence and saw Josephine standing in the
way bent over the cake, looking exactly like Grannie
as she pursed her face to drive the knife through. I
stayed stupidly looking, not able to get back until the
cake was cut, and although she had not noticed me
she reminded me in her spitefully unconscious vindic-
tive spoil-sport way that it was my turn to go to
Grannie's. There was no need to say it. It was part of

her everlasting internal conversation about the dark
side. Something leapt from me towards her; the room
was a sound in a dream. Life; a dream swimming in
sound. Today was still all round the pattern round the
edge of my plate, and I felt that a particular way of
putting jam on to my bread and butter would keep
everything off. But the layer went over, thinning out
over the creamy butter, raspberry jam being spread
with a trembling hand by nobody, nowhere . . . by
Josephine. The morning garden, the sunlit afternoon
heath, the eternal perfect Sunday happiness of all the
rooms in the house were Josephine's. She held them
there or snatched them away. Grannie's was woven
in her dark mind *always*; all the time.

II

The summer shone down Grannie's road in a single
wash of gold over the little yellow brick houses. Inside
her sitting-room it had gone. There was a harsh black
twilight full of the dreadful sweetish emanation that
was always in her room. It came out dreadfully from
the cold firm wrinkles of her cheek when I kissed her
and shook out over me from her draperies when she
raised her arm and patted me and made that moment
when I always forgot what I had intended to say.
When her arm came down the beads of her big oak
bracelet rattled together as the ends of her long-
boned puffy fingers patted the horsehair seat. People
sat down. I sat down, aching with my smile. Her long
stiff hands were already fumbling her ear trumpet
from the lap of her silk dress. When I had secured the

speaking end she said, how are you, my dear? Very
well, thank you – how are *you*, I shouted slowly. The
visit had begun; some of it had gone. Eh she quavered
out of the years. If she could see into the middle of my
head she would see the lawn of her old garden and the
stone vase of geraniums and calceolarias in the
bright sunlight, and would stop. Her tall figure
tottering jerkily under its large black shawldraped
dress, the lapels of her lace cap, the bony oval of her
face, the unconscious stare of her faded blue eyes as
she moved and stood about the garden all *meant*. I
was a ghost meaning nothing, then and now. She sat
wearing the same Sunday clothes but her eyes were
on my sliding silence. I said my words over again.
They were lasting longer than if she had understood
at once. Her face fell as she heard. Middling . . .
middling, she said in a shrill murmur. Isn't it a lovely
day I shouted angrily. My throat was already sore
with effort. Her disappointed eyes remained fixed on
me. It has been *lovely* today I yelled. Did your father
go she asked with a reluctant quiver. My false face
when I shouted back showed her she had misunder-
stood. She sighed and turned away from the light. The
long tube slithered in the folds of her dress as she sat
back, still holding the trumpet to her ear. Presently
she turned slowly round and lowered the trumpet and
patted my knee. I smiled and said we went for a walk,
very quietly. I felt she must be hearing. She put up the
trumpet again. I could not say it over again, she would
know what I meant if I waited. I hesitated and felt a
crimson blush. She smiled and patted my knee with
her free hand. You're growing up a bonny woman she
quavered. People having tea in basket chairs under

trees watched. The beauty of the day hammered in
the room. She saw it all. But her words were a bridge
thrown towards nothing. It gets dark earlier now
shouted my ghost. The summer's going, she quavered,
turning away again and putting down the trumpet. I
lowered the mouthpiece and she coiled the apparatus
in her lap and sat back giving her cry as her shoulders
touched the back of her chair. Bad, bad, she whispered, patting her left arm and smiling towards me. I
nodded vehemently. Listen to the minister, she
murmured, read your bible every day. She sighed
heavily and sat thinking of us all one by one. About us
in the foreground of her thoughts was her large old
house and our small one. It was long before she came
back to her small home near our big one. I turned
away from her heavy fragile thinking profile when I
reached the moment of hoping that the end would
come here so that she might never bring the trumpet
and the chapel magazines to make a centre of gloom
in amongst everything. When I looked again her
heavy thin profile gleamed whiter in the deepening
light. I could no longer see the little frayed blue veins.
I looked about the room. The furniture was death-
soaked. It knew only of lives lived fearing death. I
looked at Grannie again. My tingling hands touched a
thought . . . The loud beating of my heart filled space.
Lord. Lord Christ. Mr Christ. Jesus Christ, Esquire. I
had thought the thought . . . Below the joys and
wonders of my life was that. Me. I began social conversation eagerly towards the room, in my mind. It
went on and on fluently. I had found out how to do it.
My mind pressed against the sky and spread over the
earth discovering. I strung out thoughts in unfamiliar

phrases, laughing in advance to blind my hearers until I was safely away over bridge after bridge. I nearly bent forward to secure the speaking tube. I felt it in my hand. It was no use. It would carry my thought into action . . . All social talk was hatred. I sat twisting my fingers together longing to get back into the incessant wonders and joys away from the room that had seen my truth. The room throbbed with it. It made the room seem lighter, the twilight going backward, evening and gaslight never to come . . . When the gaslight *came* on the furniture the room would become quiet and harmless again . . . It was dark and cold. Voices were sighing and moaning through the walls. The hell waiting for me *made* the wonders and joys . . . it might come soon; any day. Who can tell how oft he offendeth. Cleanse thou me from secret faults. Useless. God was not greater than I. The force of evil is as great and eternal as the force of good . . . I wanted to cast myself on my knees and weep aloud in anger. Be angry and sin not. That meant waiting meanly for the good things to come back. There were no good things. If God saw and knew evil he was evil . . . Grannie sighed. I smiled towards her through the twilight, my body breaking into a refreshing dew. The little room was being folded in darkness. The bright light that came into it in the morning was a stranger; a new light. Light the gas, dearie, whispered Grannie. Years slipped in and out as the gaslight spread its gold wings sideways from its core of blue. The evening stretched across the room, innocently waiting.

CHRISTMAS EVE

I PUT down my pilgrim basket and went into the office for Miss Barron's welcome. It was Miss Spencer, in one of her older dresses, writing a letter at the office table. It was too late to alter my expression.

'*Well*, dear lady, this is *very* charming.' She kept her pen in her hand as she spoke.

I had been going to say to Miss Barron I wanted to come.

I laughed uneasily and stood waiting half-way between the door and the table. If I could not quickly find something to say she would at least be asking me to read prayers in the morning.

'Very charming,' she repeated, putting an elbow on the table and removing her pince-nez.

I muttered shapelessly that I was taking refuge because I had so many invitations, and thought if I had an engagement here nobody would be offended.

'What an excellent plan . . . *Isn't* it difficult to keep one's friends from being jealous of each other? Isn't it a *problem*. Well, we're charmed to have you here – *Oh*, we've had such a day, dear lady.'

I beamed insincere curiosity and murmured that she didn't look it.

'Well, it's all over now. All's well that ends well. Weren't you surprised to find the front door unlocked?'

I hurriedly agreed, privately inferring it must be later than I thought. Edith would be putting in time in the common room. She would think I had backed out.

'I say, have you had supper? Have you been journeying?'

I had had a meal.

'Right. Well, sit down a moment before you go upstairs. I *must* tell you our story. D'you mind shutting the door . . . Do you remember Fraulein *Braun*? Of course you do. She was here in the summer. Yes, that's the lady. Did you? Well, perhaps it's going ahead in Germany more quickly than we think; if many more of the women are like her. You *ought* to have been here about an hour ago; about ten o'clock. Well. I *must* just give you the story in outline. It's so exceptional. I think you'll be interested . . . It all began *yesterday*. I thought there was something wrong with her about tea-time. She looked the picture of dejection. You know there's nothing like a foreigner when they are dejected. Is there? . . . No. Yes, that's it, isn't it extraordinary? Well; it seems she had been counting on the arrival of a little Christmas tree from Germany. Miss Barron tells me she had talked about it for days; and after this morning's post she began to *despair*. *Oh*, we've had such a day with her. She wandered about the house and kept on coming down to the hall and staring out through the vestibule and muttering to herself. *I* was afraid we should have

her ill. Can you imagine – such an intelligent woman
and – well – I suppose thirty, shouldn't you say?' I
suggested that they thought a good deal of Christmas.

'*She* does certainly. It was *really awful*. I think any
of us would have given up our parcels only too willingly to put an end to her misery. Well, the climax
came after this evening's post. The nine o'clock postman came at ten. She was standing silently waiting on
the stairs. I assure you I didn't know how to face her
empty-handed. I wish you could have been there. It
had its funny side, you know. I said I'm afraid your
parcel hasn't come Fraulein Braun. She didn't move.
She just stood still on the stairs and said in a loud
voice – 'I go out – to buy a tree.' At ten-fifteen; on
Christmas Eve. I saw at once it would be perfectly
useless to try and stop her. She would have defied me.
And I knew she would not come back until she had
found one. So I had to fling X.Y. rules to the winds and
let her go forth . . . I sent Miss Banks with her. She's
pretty level-headed and knows her way about London
. . . I've never had such an experience in the whole of
my time. Fortunately they're nearly all away.'

I admired the excitement.

'*Excitement*, dear lady – I *was* anxious until they
came back. I was never so glad to see anyone in my
life.'

'When did they come?'

'At eleven; just before you did. They found a tree in
Lisson   Grove – *Lisson   Grove*.   She   came   back
beaming. Came in here holding it up in the air, poor
Bankie at her last gasp in the background. She says
Fraulein *ran* along the streets *crying*, and rushed into
the green-grocers' shops hardly able to speak. Well.

That's not the end. I thought we were well over our troubles when I saw her with the tree. But no. She stood over me – you know how tall she is, and said, 'I must have matches.' She had bought a little box of coloured candles! I tried to dissuade her diplomatically. She simply said, 'It is useless: I must have matches.' I had to give in. So she's gone off to her cubicle with her matches and I've put off turning out time until eleven forty-five. Did you ever hear anything like it? I've warned her room not to go to their cubicles till half past and I've asked her to keep the curtains withdrawn. What do you suppose she is doing?'

'Oh, she'll light up and be satisfied. It's rather charming.'

'It'll be very charming if she sets the house on fire. I think it's too comic. One person, with a Christmas tree, in a cubicle. Don't say anything in the common room. There are a few wild spirits not gone home and a good many strangers.'

I recognised only a few faces. The Greens and Eunice were sitting with their workboxes and under-linen in their usual talking row on the settee facing the fire. Little Green had put up her hair. 'Hullo, ghost; here's a ghost,' she said. I greeted them vaguely and passed on to the centre of the room. Edith was sitting over a book at the far table beneath the windows with her back to the room. I paused under the lights with an open letter, to take in the other groups about the fire. Two women, a mother and daughter, the provincial X.Y. type, reading bibles. In the largest armchair a tiny Hindu sitting upright, the firelight gleaming on the gold threads of her striped draperies. She was listening and smiling gently into vacancy. Her tiny hands clasped on her knees looked social, as if they had never been alone. Near her sat Miss Banks. The heavy scroll of her profile hung over a moirette petticoat; her compressed lips and the eager hunch of her shoulders expressed her satisfaction in the tuck that would make it short enough to wear. Perhaps she had seen me come in, perhaps not. Four or five figures were grouped about the door side of the fireplace, waiting over X.Y. library books for bedtime, numbly waiting for Christmas to come and go.

'Hullo, Winged Victory,' I murmured under cover of the talk on the settee. Edith darted to her feet and stood restraining her welcome as I went wearily forward.

'Why don't you have the table light and aren't you fearfully cold?' I asked.

'No,' she whispered. 'Is it cold? Are you cold?'

'I don't know. I've just heard one of the most pathetic things I ever heard.'

'Shall we go upstairs?'

I looked vaguely about. 'It was a splendid idea of yours,' whispered Edith.

The door opened suddenly on Miss Spencer. Everyone looked round.

'Oh' – she said comprehensively. 'Will you *all* please come up to No. 8 for a few minutes. Fraulein Braun wishes us all to gather together for a few minutes. It is a German custom. I think we must all go. Will you all come? Just for a few minutes.'

Cook was the last to come in. She was wearing her ulster and had a piece of red flannel round her neck

and her usual winter expression of being in the midst
of a bad cold. The curtains were all thrown up over
their rails leaving the room clear. Someone had
pushed back the beds so that there was space on the
linoleum-covered floor for all to stand about the little
tree. Its many candles glowed sharply in the cold air.
Fraulein Braun stood near the tree as we all gathered
in a rough circle.

'What are we to do, Fraulein?' asked Miss Spencer
briskly to cover a giggle from little Green.

'Are all here?' asked Fraulein in her deep voice.

'Everyone in the house, Fraulein.'

Fraulein drew back into the awkward circle
between Edith and the little Hindu who was standing
with reverently bent head and her little hands
clasped downwards before her. At the end of a
moment Fraulein's rich voice rose and filled the large
cold room.

> 'Sh – ti – il – le *Nacht*
> Hei – li – ge *Nacht* . . .'

As she sang the room seemed to grow less cold. The
sharp separate rays of the little candles changed to
one rosy golden blur.

When Fraulein's voice ceased there was silence.
Miss Spencer looked about with a cheerful question-
ing face. She could be heard urging someone to do
something. In a moment she would speak. I was
aware of a stirring at my side and felt the flush that
made cook's face uniform with her nose. Her impulse
had animated more than one, but it was her old
unused voice that broke the silence with song in
which presently all joined as they could:

'While shepherds watched their flocks by night
      All seated on the ground,
The Angel of the Lord came down,
      And glory shone around.'

SLEIGH RIDE

AND now the thin penetrating mist promised increasing cold. The driver flung on a cloak, secured at the neck but falling open across his chest and leaving exposed his thinly clad arms and bare hands.

She pulled high the collar of her fur coat, rimy now at its edges, and her chin ceased to ache and only her eyes and cheekbones felt the thin icy attacking mist that had appeared so suddenly. The cold of a few moments ago numbing her face had brought a hint of how one might freeze quietly to death, numbed and as if warmed by an intensity of cold; and that out amongst the mountains it would not be terrible. But this raw mist bringing pain in every bone it touched would send one aching to one's death, crushed to death by a biting increasing pain.

She felt elaborately warm, not caring even now how long might go on this swift progress along a track that still wound through corridors of mountains and still found mountains rising ahead. But night would come and the great shapes all about her would be wrapped away until they were a darkness in the sky.

If this greying light were the fall of day, then certainly the cold would increase. She tried to reckon how far she had travelled eastwards, by how much earlier the sun would set. But south, too, she had come . . .

The mist was breaking, being broken from above. It dawned upon her that they had been passing impossibly through clouds and were now reaching their fringe. Colour was coming from above, was already here in dark brilliance, thundery. Turning to look down the track she saw distance, cloud masses, light-soaked and gleaming.

And now from just ahead, high in the sky, a sunlit peak looked down.

Long after she had sat erect from her warm ensconcement the sunlit mountain corridors still seemed to be saying watch, see, if you can believe it, what we can do. Always it seemed that they must open out and leave her upon the hither side of enchantment, and still they turned and brought fresh vistas. Sungilt masses beetling variously up into pinnacles that truly cut the sky high up beyond their high-clambering pinewoods, where their snow was broken by patches of tawny crag. She still longed to glide forever onwards through this gladness of light.

But the bright gold was withdrawing. Presently it stood only upon the higher ridges. The colour was going and the angular shadows, leaving a bleakness of white, leaving the mountains higher in their whiteness. One there towered serene, that seemed at its top to walk up the deepening blue, a sharply flattened cone aslant, pure white. She watched it, its thickness of snow, the way from its blunted tower it came broadening down unbroken by crag, radiant white until far down its pinewoods made a little gentleness about its base. Up there on the quiet of its top-most angle it seemed there must be someone, minutely rejoicing in its line along the sky.

A turn brought peaks whose gold had turned to rose. She had not eyes enough for seeing. Seeing was not enough. There was sound, if only one could hear it, in this still, signalling light.

The last of it was ruby gathered departing upon the topmost crags, seeming, the moment before it left them, to be deeply wrought into the crinkled rock.

At a sharp bend the face of the sideways lounging driver came into sight, expressionless.

'Schön, *die letzte Glüh*,' he said quietly.

When she had pronounced her 'Wunderschön,' she sat back released from intentness, seeing the scene as one who saw it daily; and noticed then that the colour ebbed from the mountains had melted in the sky. It was this marvel of colour, turning the sky to a molten rainbow, that the driver had meant as well as the rubied ridges that had kept the sky forgotten.

Just above a collar of snow, that dipped steeply between the peaks it linked, the sky was a soft green-ish purple paling upwards from mauve-green to green whose edges melted imperceptibly into the deepening blue. In a moment they were turned towards the opposite sky, bold in smoky russet rising to amber and to saffron-rose expanding upwards; a high radiant background for its mountain, spread like a banner, not pressed dense and close with deeps strangely moving, like the little sky above the collar.

The mountain lights were happiness possessed, sure of recurrence. But these skies, never to return, begged for remembrance.

The dry cold deepened, bringing sleep. Drunk, she felt now, with sleep; dizzy with gazing, and still there was no sign of the end. They were climbing a narrow track between a smooth high drift, a greying wall of snow, and a precipice sharply falling.

An opening; the floor of a wide valley. Mountains hemming it, exposed from base to summit, moving by as the sleigh sped along the level to where a fenced road led upwards. Up this steep road they went in a slow zigzag that brought the mountains across the way now right now left, and a glimpse ahead, against the sky, of a village, angles and peaks of low buildings sharply etched, quenched by snow, crushed between snow and snow, and in their midst the high snow-shrouded cone of a little church; Swiss village, lost in wastes of snow.

At a tremendous pace they jingled along a narrow street of shops and chalets that presently opened to a circle about the little church and narrowed again and ended, showing beyond, as the sleigh pulled up at the steps of a portico, rising ground and the beginning of pinewoods.

SUMMER

I

ARE we really going? Is it settled?
Laura knew all the details. She was pleased
and excited, but she told me about it as she might tell
a favourite pupil.

Do you *realise* that tomorrow we shall be in the
heart of the country? I said in her first pause.

Mps, dearie, of course I do, she said, without lifting
her face from her darning. Down there she would be
exactly the same; pleased and excited and steady,
with her fingers at someone's needlework whenever
we were not actually out. Wish I was in some other
heart, too, she said presently. The Sunday school
master at Broadstairs. Sunday school masters were
as sly and self-protective as other men. I went on
excitedly talking until the dewy balm that had come
into the twilight while Laura spoke had disappeared.
It would come back when we were in the country.
Whenever they were all busily talking.

The folding doors opened and Beads looked in,

surveying us. The uneasiness of not offering to go and
help disappeared as soon as the doors had closed
behind Laura and Beads. It was in them, not in me and
the room. It might come back when we were all
together at supper. But it was so much more important to realise the wonder of going on anywhere, from
Brussels. The first days came back now in full force;
the light that was on them flowed forward through
the whole past month, and the wonder of tonight
hemmed in by tomorrow's move flowed back to the
beginning . . . This evening of all evenings I was alone
with the room for the first time. And because I was not
busy with the others, someone was *seeing* the glimmer
of the hot twilight on the polished floor, and over the
dark old furniture and up the old high polished doors,
and seeing how the candles drooped even further than
yesterday over the sides of their sconces. The climax
of the hot week was not being missed.

There might be a storm tonight. Perhaps tomorrow
Brussels might be cool again, as at the beginning . . .
In the country we should walk together down dusty
roads with nothing to distract our attention from each
other, and not even the excitement of the fearful sul-
try heat. But there would be cool sleep.

II

The morning was hotter. Aunt Lillie apologised for
coming to breakfast in curling pins. I caused quite a
lot of conversation about the weather. They were all
puffing and complaining and none of us had slept
much, but I was so happy in the thought of the cool

country nights that although I knew I looked more
shiny and straight-haired than anyone, I was able to
talk; moist, marshy heat, the most trying there is, a
little like the heat of a jungle; the heat of a jungle on a
small scale; I was not trying to put anyone right, so the
aunts were not offended. That just expresses it, they
said, and were grateful and approving, as they would
have been with a man. But the conversation was soon
turned to the details of the journey, and I could see
that everyone was seeing it as a social function, to be
got through creditably. I had never before thought of
a journey as an affair with strange people looking on
all the time, criticising your things. If I pretended, and
saw it in their way all the time I might be popular all
day, but the journey would be missed. There were an
enormous number of dreadful too-late things to be
done before we could start; I undertook to get a cloth-
ball in French at the chemist's near by, and went out
directly after breakfast, alone for the first time in
Brussels. *Charcuterie; estaminet; pharmacien;* I
walked up and down the rue where these shops stood
with houses in between them. They were real and my
own for the first time; and the Avenue Louise real in
the distance each time I came up the street. Each time
I turned and went back looking on the sunlit morning
pavement I saw picture after picture: the white mar-
ble reredos at Lißege; the high façade of Louvain
Cathedral; a strange echoing street of high, flat-
fronted houses in Malines; Bruges façades standing at
angles to each other in different lights, unfathomable
lacework in stone shutting you in for ever; the ever-
green stretch of Waterloo from the top of the many
steps; the flowered embroidery backs of the priests at

high mass in Ste Gudule, the steep of the Rue Montagne de la Cour; the festival of Sainte Marie at Laeken; the perspiring priests carrying the image of the Virgin under a canopy. If all those things could come back, perhaps tomorrow's journey would also come back. However miserable I was, I could not be more miserable than I had been in all those places.

I knew we should miss the train. It was starting just as Laura and I reached the platform. I felt desperate. We ran along the platform towards a little dark man with a blue-black beard and a metal-edged cap shouting, and pointing towards the five aunts running down the incline. Beads and Mousie joined us laughing. The train stopped.

III

It was evening when we got to the last junction. Laura and I had been sitting in the middle places of a third class carriage. It was crowded with peasants. The general smelliness was healthy. I tried to tell Laura their clothes do not smell like the clothes of English poor people. They give out a smell of life. She said, I say, dear, Aunt Lillie left her sketch block behind after all, and laughed towards the young man in the corner, making him notice her, and yet she is much more religious than I am. The air began coming in as they all got out. At first it was like fine needles against your face. There was something dark in the sky behind the station. I jumped out of the carriage and ran forward a few steps. I could hardly stop. The pine scent in the air lifted my hair and made all my body free of my clothes. The darkness behind the station was a *mountain*. There were mountains all about. We were in a sort of gorge. Did they know it was like this? We got into another hot train, but we had two carriages to ourselves with a low partition between, and leaned out of the windows. The train went slowly along. It was getting lighter. The sky behind the mountains was sharp with light. I thought the end of the world might be coming. I went across to Beads and Laura, and said something. Beads turned round from leaning out of the window and looked surprised, and said it was ripping. I turned back towards the light. It was a large silver-gold moon, hanging in a cleft. Two slopes went up on either side spiked with pine-trees. Before the end of the journey the moon was up above the low mountains. Their shapes went slowly by. I remembered that I had not seen mountains before. But when I called back the moment of seeing them, they had always been there. They were *there*; they had come out of me into the sky; a part of me that I knew, in the sky. At one place there was a white torrent flowing down. I leaned out and heard the rush of it. The air rushed over my face.

IV

The inside of the inn seemed brown. Its whitewashed walls were rich with the brown of knotty, rough, stained woodwork, and brilliant white in the lamplight. Upstairs large rooms opened out of each other. I thought the walls were brown as we went in and out, but it was again the rich brown woodwork of

the doors and windows against the white walls, and
there was a brown crucifix on a wall of each room.
Wherever you looked there were white walls lit by
brown in different lights as people moved their candles. Everyone was talking in happy excited voices,
going in and out of the rooms. When we went down to
supper I was the last. The corridor had two high,
immense windows, nearly up to its ceiling. Moonlight
poured through them on to the floor. The ceiling was
invisible in darkness. I stood still. They ought to have
stopped here. Roland came back and came across the
floor and quickly kissed my cheek. You mustn't forget
I am your cousin, he apologised, drumming his fists
together. He was quite right though, there, at that
moment. Downstairs we all sat round a round white
wooden table. There were petits pains and farm butter, and a gaufre and a large soft ball of cream cheese
sprinkled with caraway seeds.

V

The sheets were pale brownish yellow, and very
coarse. They smelt of pine. When the candles were
out and the sounds had ceased the pine scented air
came in more strongly.

VI

I thought we were to be in the village a week. But at
breakfast they blotted everything out with the guide
official and arranged something for every day. There

was only one morning for the village. The inn was in a green lane, like an English lane, but a little way down it turned and ran up the hill. A little way up the hill a little white plaster church stood on a green level. Bright sunlight poured over it. The hills moved higher into the sky as we went towards them; their bases opened out, altering the landscape as we went. Pine clad hills moved behind the church as we came. There was a blue and pink Madonna above the peaked porch. Incense came through the open door into the strong air, bringing eternal happiness. It was not strange mountain scenery. It was Belgium. The happy, holy scent of Belgium mingled with the pine scented air.

VII

We all went upstairs and stood concealed behind our window curtains. Dark figures were trooping in line up the little hill. In front, just behind the coffin, a slight wispy figure staggered and plunged along, two solid figures holding her arms on either side. It was from her the terrible cries were coming. I could not believe it. They ought not to let her go . . . The cries died away into the little church. There was silence again, but the cries seemed to resound and fill the sunlit landscape . . . They were the *right* cries; the *outbreak* of grief; not in a room; full and free out there in the sun, where she used to talk to him. They went out over the mountains explaining the songs of the birds and the happiness and beauty everywhere.

NOOK ON PARNASSUS

DRAWING incredulously nearer, I felt the fathom-
less preoccupations of marketing fall away and
vanish.

Five, clipped together, one below the other, down
the centre of the little window I had passed, almost
daily, for months, aware of what it held, seeing what
it held without needing to look. Today, summoning my
eyes as I approached, these magnetic newcomers
whose immediate gift – a sense of eternity in hand to
spend as I chose – had set me free to pause and stare
my adoration, soon turned them to search amongst
their neighbours for a possible solution of the mystery
of their own arrival amongst things able to evoke only
the consciousness of passing the unvarying contents
of a stationer's shop window.

Right and left hung limp floralities, executed
entirely in half-witted pastel shades, unchildlike
children, draped in floating films and posed, in the
attitudes of dancing, amidst vegetation whose improb-
ability was unredeemed by any touch of magic; trucu-
lent gnomes, self-consciously gesticulating from the

tops of inanimate toadstools. Above, in a row, the customary photographs: frozen Royalties with unseeing eyes, alternating with Stars whose eyes saw only that which so eagerly they invited the observer to observe. Below, the usual piles, zigzag, of Bond and Club this and that; envelopes to match.

Returning to my captors, I wondered along what pathway these five solitaries, keeping each other such splendid company, had reached the frame whence they offered me, in addition to the joy of their mere presence, a solution, easily and most blessedly at hand within the radius of a brief shopping round, the perfect solution of an annually recurrent problem. In size, they were comfortably larger than postcards and, no doubt, conspicuously thicker. Altogether more imposing, even when emerging, plain side uppermost, from their envelopes – I made a mental note of the special envelopes – than those perfect close-ups of west-country seagulls last year delighting so many of my urban friends.

Thankfully banishing 'C.c.' from the formidable list of tasks to be fulfilled before I left town, I entered the shop.

Its counter repeated the appeals of its window, minus my treasures. Behind it appeared, coming forward from a dim background, the diminutive elderly woman still occasionally to be found attending the counters of small shops. The style of her dress, like that of her hair, or wig, a compact chignon, imperfectly dyed and most intricately braided, had been carried forward from the last century, together with her attitude towards a postulant customer, represented by the beam, vivid as a spark amidst dying

ashes, whose mingling of craftily rapacious adoration and ill-contained impatience of the necessary
ritual of salesmanship, reached me with the force of a
personal assault.

By what means had she acquired, or been per-
suaded into acquiring, that inappropriate quintet?

'You have some reproductions in the window,' I
began, and saw the projected beam die out, leaving
the eyes disgustedly surveying one of those customers
who waste an hour selecting a twopenny card.

' 'Ere they are,' she muttered indifferently, lifting a
yellowish claw in the direction of a winged pillar
standing close at hand upon the crowded counter.
With a murmur of apology, I turned to flip the revolving wings and find them composed, indeed, of the
whole company, Stars, and gnomes, Royalties and
fairy-footed children.

'Yes,' I said appreciatively, 'but you have some
others, in the window – German reproductions of
French masters.'

Her uncertain pursuit of these technicalities ended,
after a moment's reflection during which her eyes,
grown round and almost gentle, became as thoughtful
and detached as those of a meditating doctor, ended in
a smile expressing both amusement and relief.

'Aow – *them*!'

While bustling along to escape from behind the
counter, she pointed eagerly towards the space
beyond me. Swinging round, I found them, laid out
upon a small table: the window quintet and several
others, waiting to be apprehended, one by one. Wondering, as I faced her collection, whether I ought,
penitently, to revise my estimate, I found her at my

side, aware of my appreciative concentration and, in a moment, aware also of the desirability of offering a little assistance, if its desired result were to be achieved within a reasonable time.

'That's a pretty one,' she said encouragingly, pointing to Dürer's immortal nosegay, grown in a world familiar with 'vilets, penny-a-bunch', so oddly modern and so quaintly commonplace, and added, after a moment's endurance of my silence and of the flow of time, during which, taking in, out here in the open, the presence of a weather-stained mackintosh and an ancient shopping bag, she had become uncertain as to the ultimate descent of the fruit dangling tantalisingly before her eyes: 'Sixpence each,' revealing the secret of her earlier change of mood and manner, and leaving the other secret, the link between herself and these new items of her stock, still to be fathomed.

'I must look at them all,' I said, putting in time, and added, aching to be rid of her, unable while she remained, alien and unsharing at my side, even to investigate, still less gaze my fill: 'Are these all you have?'

Muttering, she turned away so abruptly as to carry my unoccupied eyes to her retreating form, soon reaching a frosted door at the back of the shop, through which emerged, the moment it was opened and while still my side-tracked consciousness struggled with the problem of reckoning a total of forty-five sixpences, the radiant explanation of the mystery.

Her smock, the colour of a ripe orange, ardently supporting the red-gold of her bushed hair, may or may not have been the one worn during the final term of her course at the school of Art, whose lamentable sequel, inconceivable when first she had passed within its alluring door, she was now trying to redeem by introducing, amongst the detested wares of a sceptical employer, these radiant aliens. But the expression leaping to the eyes that met my own the moment before she advanced, slowly and with a trifle too much elegance, as if fastidiously picking her way through an unworthy universe, may well have inhabited them on the day she left that door for the last time, and now, temporarily restored by the vision of a customer standing before her miniature exhibition and therefore capable of paying tribute where she herself knew it to be due, was revealing, helplessly, and none the less pathetically for one's admiring certainty of her having come forth sternly self-propelled by intelligent appreciation of the depth and range of her insufficiency, the torment she had endured while being weighed in the balance and found wanting.

Within the depths of my embarrassment, I sought about for means of congratulating her, for some means of conveying an instanteously improvised idea: that every factory and shop in the kingdom should thankfully retain upon its staff at least one student of art. But when she reached my side and we stood together confronted by her gods, my desire to share, to take her by the arm and say, quietly and chummily, 'Aren't they heavenly?' was checked by the chill aloofness reigning within her assumed air of courteous availability. I said, instead:

'I want some of these for Christmas cards, and it's almost impossible to choose,' and immediately felt curious, even eager, to know which of the set, if she really felt she were being leaned upon, she would proceed to select.

'Yes.'

The single word came forth so compactly, and the manner accompanying it, a faintly supercilious detachment, so clearly expressed her indifference to my dilemma that my thoughts retired upon the witness in the background, surely at this moment preparing atorrid discourse upon the subject of dealing with hesitant customers.

'Quite a number of D'yawrers,' I hazarded, beginning, according to my plan – evolved while I realised, unless indeed this convenient shop should vanish, or its new feature, together with its new assistant, should disappear, that it would supply any number of solutions of the C.c. problem, provided I took, each year, sufficient multiples of only one card – of choice by gradual elimination, at the last row.

'The Dürers are nice,' she breathed, giving to the name a slight prominence and, to myself, unholy joy over her fragment of delight in parading correctitude, and joy, equally unholy, in recalling my own pride in a perfect pronounciation of foreign names; pride that was to die a painless, natural death in association with those amongst whom my knowledge and appreciation of the pictures by whose ghosts we were confronted, had been born and had gradually become inseparable from the comfortably anglicised form of the names of their creators. Wondering whether, in these days of universal travel, the youngest generation of art students were mostly linguists, I went on up my rows, again, in my entrancement, abandoning my ape-like ability to reproduce every sort of native sound until, once again, she rebuked me.

'Toolooze-*Low*treck,' I had murmured, 'Gogang . . . van Go . . . Mannay. Impossible to choose.'

Immediately upon the end of my despairing sigh, came her voice, quiet and very clear:

'Toulouse-Lautrec is charming.' 'Dashing and elegant,' I countered, and blushed to the soul for my cruelty. 'M'yes,' she retorted irritably and drove hurriedly onward: 'the Mahnehs, too . . .' 'Overwhelming. They come for you with both fists.'

'Oh,' she simpered disdainfully – recalling perhaps, the silencing of some extravagant youngster by an assertion from on high to the effect that a picture is a picture and is either, for various ascertainable reasons, hard to learn, 'but that is what you are here for,' a good or a bad picture – and murmured, with the hint in her voice of a malicious smile: '*Not* then, very suitable for your purpose.'

This would not do at all. This brawling in church must cease, or the card I selected would be under a curse. Dumbly, hesitantly, I extended a random finger, hoping for some kind of unity.

'Gaugin,' she breathed, relenting, 'is *always* wonderful.' ('Powerfully averted and inverted,' I amended, but succeeded in preventing the words from reaching the battlefield.) 'But perhaps, for your purpose, this particular van Goch . . .' Is the gutteral quite so Scotch I wondered, and then realised with relief that she had reached the end of her little exhibition. Whichever I should proceed to choose there were no more names to pronounce and, since mercifully she had not distracted my attention by giving this artist an inappropriate label, there was now no barrier to unity, born suddenly between us of the happiness of her choice. This sufficiently applauded, and her agreement almost secured for my proclamation of a sunlit kitchen garden, crowded from side to side with buoyant vegetables, as eminently suited to greet the eye at the darkest moment of the year, we turned to settle the question of the envelopes and, although the movements of her hands about the counter expressed both uncertainty and the distaste inspired by the processes to be mastered in the course of 'learning the business', we had soon found a perfect fit.

But the little old lady, again to the fore and watchful, immediately pounced. 'Too thin,' she ruled, with eager scorn. 'These are what you want. Ninepence the packet.'

Though well aware that the old wretch was trading upon my delight, I meekly sought my purse. By the time I had solved this second problem in mental arithmetic, the girl had vanished. Frostily, I paid for my one card and the many envelopes. Perhaps when I called for the rest of the cards, truly, I reflected on her behalf, a handsome order, I might meet my little friend again.

Reaching the street, and again surveying the window, I discerned in a remote corner a mall notice: 'Artists' Materials.' Behind it stood a bundle of pencils and a roll of Whatman. A new line, for the little woman's little shop, whose items were by her considered insufficiently tasty to appear amongst the gnomes, fairies and Bonds. And the young woman, newly at work on the first job that had offered, and trying at least to be a door-keeper in the house of Art, had scored, this afternoon, her first triumph over her employer's incredulity?

TRYST

GOODNESS! Nearly teatime, and nothing ready. She felt deliciously refreshed. Brief, sweet sleep had drawn away the fever of weariness possessing her when she had collapsed into the great armchair.

But already it must be too late even to pop outside.

Yet she found herself hurrying, eager, thinking of the open, as if, by the time all was ready, it still might not be too late. After all, the promise she had given herself as the door slammed behind them, just before she had fallen off into that heavenly doze, given with her eyes upon Hokusai's Wave – arrived for Christmas and set up on the mantelpiece as if to remind her, with the coming of the New Year, that on any day the sea was just too far off – to go out and breathe for a few minutes the air under a sky that today stood high and clear, could, if she chose, in any case be kept. If not before tea, then after.

But there was something else. Something besides just sniffing the air. Urgent. Not stating itself.

Kitchen fire stirred up, soon to be clear enough for making toast, if they felt like making toast. Kettle on.

Tea laid in the darkening sitting-room. She glanced at the clock. In about ten minutes time they would be back.

As she stood lighting the passage lamp the wind, drawn by the opened up house, came moaning in under the seaward door to flow round her ankles.

She was free. Outside, all her own, waited the high sky, the rich, moist air. Rejoicing in the young eagerness of her hands as they flung her cloak across her shoulders, she sped through the kitchen to open the little landward door and be outside, breathing, in the stillness created by the shelter of the house.

Ah! But how *strange* that she should have known. Ten minutes ago, just as she had felt the pull of that urgent call, the moon, now clear of the horizon, huge and golden in the thin mist left by days of rain, was lifting, above the distant ridge, a ruby rim.

Too late. But still the urgency persisted, turning her away from the triumphant moon to hurry round toward the front of the house, toward the north-west wind and the sight, perhaps, of the afterglow.

Yes, there it was. Rose-opal above a ragged, smouldering cloud-bank, the remains of the pall for so long screening the sky, drawn away now and massed low along the rim of the sea. For a moment she stood picturing the sunset the window must have framed while she slept. One of the local best: Turner and Claude in collaboration.

Ten minutes in hand. About her feet patches of soft, rain-sodden moss, emerald, miming in velvet, amidst the rank grey spear-grass, the vivid green of April. All along the trodden track to the sandy alley leading down to the sea, the moss would recur.

Why hurry? The open sea, by the time she reached the sight of it, would be a mournful grey expanse sending her thoughts toward the flow of firelight, lamplight. Yet still her footsteps hastened, down and down through twilight deepened by the dense mesh of the escorting tamarisks, down and down until she reached the end of the alley and began slowly to climb the steep hiding the sea. Up and up, for nothing, away from the only half-savoured moist sweet scents of the lane. In a moment there would be the hummocky ridge, the distant cold sea. Already its sound, a dull hammering against the outer rocks, had grown more audible. Heard from the top, it would be harsh and loud and clear.

And then a hurried return, with the moon in sight again that by this time, its splendour departed, would have become a small, brilliantly polished silver disc.

Pausing to draw breath, she heard, coming up from below the steep ridge, the familiar faint winter tinkling of the little stream at work draining the inland meadows, winding to the sea along its deep gully. Forgotten.

A few more steps. There it was, the sea, darkening. Grey, deep dense grey, for now the opal had faded from the sky. Waveless grey, sheeny under the approach of moonlight, fitting the angle of the rising ground that hid the shore and the tide's edge. There it was. She here. And at this moment the three would be nearing the house. Expectant, making for the deserted house.

Turning to toil guiltily back, passing again the edge of the steep, she leaned, holding to a sturdy tussock, over and down to greet the modest stream whose small sound rang clear above the distant voice of the

sea. And felt her heart bound within her at the strange
sight of it, a thread of molten rosy gold in the gully's
deepening twilight. Lovely little wanderer; holding
festival down there, unseen, alone. Her spirit reached
down. Clearly she saw the detail of dried reed-spikes
and decaying weeds along its banks.

And then again was gazing down from her ridge,
aware only of the stream's unexpected loveliness, its
modest pride in being observed. Obscure little field
drainer, invisible unless one craned over, stagnant
and voiceless in summer and choked with weeds and
reeds, in winter dismal with their disarray, it had
called to her with its small clear voice just in time for
the display of its unaccustomed glory. Lent by the
mist that tonight was keeping for so long upon the
moon's face the glow of its rising.

Loath to part with the moment, she lingered,
counting her treasures: joy in recognising in the
transfigured runnel the bourne that so urgently had
called her forth; eager flight, down into the gully;
oblivion; and now the sure harvesting: certainty of
the moment's immortality.

With youth's elastic tread she skimmed the steeply-
rising alley. Its yellow sand was moon-paled now and
patterned with tamarisk shadows. Through the gaps
in the feathery masses she saw the moonlit distances,
the tantalising far horizons of her enclosed daily life,
accessible now, small and near, powerless to arrest
her spirit's flight.

Approaching the house, she found herself longing
for a little extra time. Time to dispose of her elas-
tically expanded being, to reassemble the faculties
demanded by the coming enclosure.

She opened the door upon the rich, warm fragrance of toasting bread, upon the adult, excited holiday voices of those who had been her babes, upon the figure of her husband advancing down the passage.

'Ah. *There* you are, my dear. A pleasant stroll? We have had an excellent walk. Excellent. Yes. And I am now engaged upon a far from excellent *search.*'

The spectacles would be where he had left them after lunch. Escape. A moment's respite while she went in search of them. Meantime, for him, unless at once she came down to earth with a spoken response, one of those silences wherein he wondered what might be wrong. 'For your specs,' she said meditatively, as though trying to think where they might be, and felt, with the sounding of her own voice, the door of her inward life close against her as surely as the house door clicked into its latch.

'Exactly. And *The Spectator*. Both, apparently, *non est.*'

And open again, as she moved away on her search, before the sound coming from without, the distant Koo-*roo*, koo-roo-roo-*roo* of a questing owl.

Crossing the room, delivering into his outstretched hands the swiftly discovered treasures, she hovered between two worlds and saw, revealed by the uneasiness wherewith he contemplated the vacuum created by the absence of her usual jest and to be crossed only by a bridge of words he must needs himself produce, the last flicker of her stricken exaltation. 'A fine day for their last,' she murmured confidentially. It was quenched, its tracks covered. And then, raising her voice:

'Toast ready, children?'

A STRANGER ABOUT

SOME good reason, sure, for police to call in on Colonel. Seems queer, though, dinner-time and rain pourin'.

'Oy, Jack!'

Young Trevelga, likely wanting something. Panting hurry he's in, too, to get home to his dinner out of the rain.

'Mornin', Terence. You'm in a grand hurry.'

'I am that, Jack. Mother said to be early, and I'm late. Run over soon as I caught sight of 'ee, for to ask can I have a lend of your sigh tonight.'

'You'm welcome. But *grass too long for mower again*, eh? Well, never mind. I know you been extra busy. But you can't sigh after dark, lad, even if rain hold up.'

'Don't mean tryin'. Morrow mornin' early, before you'm up.'

'Fine, boy. Sigh go easier when grass be wet.'

'Thankee, Jack. I'll be round for'n, then.'

'You seen sergeant on's cycle, turnin' in at Colonel Stamp's?'

'Naw, that I haven't. Why, what'll that be?'

'No much, a'reckon. Colonel, he's our JP now.'

'That's right, so he be. Reminds me, though, what you'm sayin'. There was a queer lookin' chap around dunes this mornin'. You saw 'un?'

'Before you come along, Terry, I seen just so many across dunes as I see every day. And that's nobody.'

'Eh, that's funny. I saw'n quite plain, from road. Away over. Sharumblin' along, he were, queer-like.'

'Catchin' butterflies, maybe.'

'No, Jack. That sort has nets. This one didn't have no net. Perhaps Colonel see 'im?'

'Get away, Terry. Colonel don't own dunes, no more'n we. Any one can cross over as likes.'

'Might be hidin',

'Hidin' me uncle. You get away home to your dinner, lad.'

'You'm worse'n Terry, Carnetha.'

' 'Tis all very well laughin', Jack. You've got to *think*. Nobody's safe nowadays. Nowhere.'

'You've been seein' a sight too many o' they pictures, that's what 'tis.'

' 'Tis'n the pictures, Jack. 'Tis what you *hear*. And what you read in the *papers*. There's gangsters. Now. This minute. *Everywhere*.'

'There's no gangsters here-along, don't you fear. Nothing to get; and nowhere to go when they've got it.'

'Jack. Them kind what I'm talkin' about doesn't all want to *get*. There's murderers, now. Just plain murderers. For the fun of it. *Everywhere*. You know so well as I do.'

'*Carnetha* – now. For the love o'music, keep

sensible. This man, whatever he be, he's away over dunes. You'm safe and sound. Neighbours near, and I'll be home before nightfall. It's all a bag o'nonsense, anyhow.'

'Then why do Colonel send out for sergeant?'

'Who says he sent for'n? And if he did, that's not necessary anything to do with a chap Terry thinks he saw.'

'Young Terry's eyesight's so good as yours, Jack.'

'Maybe. But I don't let me eyes run away with me head.'

'You'm a man. Things is different for you. You've got to think of me here. Alone with the children. And night comin'. If you was me, you'd think of plenty things you've no call to bother with in your strength.'

'Now, *come*, lass. Be easy. Make house vitty, the way you do, and I'll be home before there's a hope of any Mr Nobody comin' thisaway.'

With the cloam washed and put by, and a trayful sorted out for teatime, Carnetha Roseveare feels too restless to sit down as usual with her mending-basket; to sit down and *wait*. Much better bustle about and give the place an extra dusting and polishing. Find that lost piece of Ruth's new jigsaw puzzle.

The sounds of her activities come to her this afternoon as if they were being made by someone else. As if she and the whole world were hearing someone busily at work in her cottage, challenging the lurking fear. A good cottage it is, sure enough. Worth looking after, and here I am looking after'n and everybody knows it, right out through the world. Good, it do make you feel, even if you'm getting tired, to be makin' everything in the place tidy and clean. Maybe that's what minister do mean when he says cleanliness be next to godliness? But be it? What about Mrs Ipps? Forever scourin' and scrubbin' enough to deafen the neighbours and not a good word for anybody. And Mrs Trenouth with a cottage more like a pigsty and good and kind to every soul. Laughin' and kind always. Who knows what's true? Who knows? Perhaps Jack be right. Perhaps the man is just a poor fellow with nowhere to go. Silly to keep on thinking about'n.

But when at last she sits down to her sewing in the stillness of the orderly home, she feels her fear return with new power. The cottage, its every room clear to her inward eye in a single glance, seems no longer her own, belongs to itself. To the madman making his way towards the village. Rubbish. The village is safe, day-time-safe with folks about. The cottage is safe. And her own. Her mind goes back, seeing it as it was when she and Jack were furnishing. Every day more precious and wonderful. As time went by, the treasure had changed, revealed defects, inconveniences, ceaseless demands; some of them like those of a permanent invalid.

Oh, to feel sure! To have it safely back, unthreatened, never again to be thought of as burden and bondage.

Stillness becomes unendurable. Better set the table. Soon the children will be home. Their chatter'll drive away this awful quiet. But they'll add, poor little dears, to the fear. Both of them afraid. If only that old clabberjaw hadn't met 'em dinner-time, tellin' 'm what her Terry told her, and likely more, I might easier hold on to meself instead of feelin' 'm waitin' same as I be. And if only we wasn't the first cottage, and separate. Perhaps this very minute, with the light goin', he'm peerin' down lane.

From the kitchen, with kettle coming to the boil, she hears the girls run in with their happy noise. Glad to be out of school, glad to be home with Saturday holiday comin'. Likely they've forgot.

Over their tea, Thealie chatters and chatters, telling about new teacher and her new ways. A proper little mimic is Thealie. Not kind the way Ruthie is kind; not lookin' pleased like Ruthie is lookin' because Winnie Hawken's dreadful warts is sent away sudden by old Grannie Vardoe after doctor tried for weeks past to cure'n with that cruel burnin' acid and done no good. But Ruthie isn't talkin' like she mostly do. Whenever Thealie stops, she'm lookin' about room as if she'm thinkin'. Like as if she was just goin' to ask somethin'. But Thealie goes on and on with her chatter.

Going down the dark passage to call Ruth in from the back garden to help clean the pilchards, Carnetha sees her younger daughter at the open front door, foot on doorstep, brushing her shoes. Braver she is, little Thealie, than Ruth. But supposin' he was to come sudden up the path behind her? Rubbish. He ain't comin'. And out here at the back all looks safe and belonging. Sun'll strike here tomorrow after nightdark be gone. Jack'll be home before the dark come.

'There you be, my dear. Come you in now and help mother wash and clean pilchards ready to cook.'

'Eh! What – be – THAT?'

The resounding slam of the front door is followed

by Ruth's voice, with fear in it, crying out as she shoots the bolt: 'Mother! The man's in the garden! I heard'n down at gate!'

'Ruth! Shut back door and bolt'n, and go you both into kitchen and draw curtains!'

Speeding on soundless feet into the front room, she latches its window, switches the curtains together and leaves it, already alien and lost, to await the fearful owner. Running back down the passage, she joins the girls in the kitchen, dark now in the curtained twilight, draws them with trembling hands down on to the old settee, one on each side of her. No sound in life now but the in and out of panting breaths.

Come, Jack, oh, come before it be too late.

A minute or two gone. Is he on the flower-bed under the front window? Be the catch secure? Will he come round to the back, find the little window with no catch?

'Eh, here you be, Jack. What be wrong, up to your place?'

'Wrong? What do 'ee mean?'

'Well, I don't rightly know. Thinkin' you'd be back, I called round for to fetch sigh. Saw your Ruth bendin' over doorstep. When gate clicked, she fair fell into door, slammed'n, yelled somethin' fierce, and shot bolt. When I got up to door, all was quiet. Could'n hear no sound. No light anywheres. Nor no answer when I tapped. So I come on up road, thinkin' to meet 'ee. Why, what's up with 'ee, Jack?'

'Come on, ha-ha, Terry, lad. You come on, ha-ha-

ha – wi' me. Oh, me godmothers and godfathers, ha-ha-ha-*ha*!'

The sudden peremptory tattoo on the front door brings Carnetha's heart into her throat. Then the sound of the voice urgently shouting her name is so high and so strange that even as she speeds down the passage she doubts.

'Be it you, Jack?'

'Of *course* it be me.' Laughter, this time, choking the silly, blessed voice. All very well for men to laugh.

'Terry, lad,' gasped the voice as the door comes open, 'you'll find sigh in shed.'

And then he tumbles in door, like as if he'd had too much, staggers into sitting-room, plomps hisself into chair, and fair shakes roof. Wipes his eyes and goes off again. With the girls standing by, giggling their fear into nowhere.

All very *well*, for men and children.

'Get away-*do*, Jack. Fish'll be ready before you'm washed.'

ORDEAL

WHEN the taxi stopped, Agatha jumped out and gave gave the man money, evidently held ready in her hand all the way, and probably too much, to avoid a halt.

And when the lady in charge of the office asked if she were to send any telegrams, Agatha lost her head and stumbled over the address. Fan saw clearly then into her mind, the images it had held while she had talked so glibly in the cab.

In the hall she was even more unnerving. Really, it was hopeless of her, just before her farewell hug, to let her eyes stray and find a nurse happening to pass, and recoil. Result of her recent too strenuous mental exercise. Truly it was a blessing she was not coming upstairs . . .

Before Fan could recover from the spectacle of Agatha departing, to suffer all that her simple imagination and her inarticulateness in combination could force upon her, the lady in charge caught her with a remark to which she responded almost in Agatha's own manner; rushing wastefully outside herself into an obedient caricature of the speaker: in this case brusque and preoccupied, the fashion of one with mind alert and eyes all round the head. And was obliged, since the maid appearing at her side to take her suitcase had been a witness, to keep to this manner when she stepped out of the lift almost into the arms of a tall sister behind whom was waiting a short nurse.

She felt herself a guest being passed from hand to hand without release – being entertained. And indeed, for a moment, by each fresh face and fresh immediately revealed personality she *was* entertained. But she could not flatter herself into believing that these entertaining officials were themselves entertained. For them each visible hair of her head did not, as did theirs for her, stand out, a single separate mystery. If they felt anything at all it was relief, in finding that number seven had at her disposal as much manner as they. Their planned continuous engagement of her attention was very 'psychological' – horribly wise, feminine. It had created for her a miniature past in this house, and when presently she was shut up alone in her room, undressing, she did not feel a stranger there. The room had stated itself while she was talking with the sister and nurse, and was now a known room. It seemed long ago that Agatha had gone away through the hall.

She had thought in advance that her sense of personal life must cease when she entered the door of the nursing home. But instead it was intensified, as if, brought up against a barrier from behind which no certain future poured into it, her life flowed back upon itself, embarrassing her with its vivid palpitation. Her known self, arrested thus, was making all its statements at once. The most welcome was its cheerfulness, inexplicable and as little expected as the wise-seeming state of composure that had risen unsummoned during the last two days, like a veil between herself and her knowledge of her lack of courage. That was negative, acceptance of the inevitable. But there was nothing negative in this deep, good cheer that made her smile as she hung up her garments in a wardrobe, perhaps for the last time. It was not stoicism. It might be unconscious organic certainty of getting through. In her conscious mind was no certainty but that of the life-risk. Perhaps that itself was the invigorating factor. Whatever its cause, this present intensity of being made the possible future look like a shallow expanse; something very easy to sacrifice if she considered only herself. And those others out in life seemed now to call for solicitude only because they did not know how strange was the being in which they were immersed.

Very carefully she arranged her hair, firmly putting in extra pins, being back while she did so within the final moments of arranging herself for parties in her girlhood. And all the time the lugubrious thoughts and anticipations belonging to the occasion, and so fertile in her mind a week ago, seemed hovering in the background seeking in vain for space to intervene.

The short nurse brought the cup of thin soup that was breakfast and lunch, left hurriedly promising to come back in a moment, and came, with her already so well known way of opening the door – a quiet, wide flourish that showed the whole of her at once, arm outstretched by hand holding door knob.

They were all trained of course, Fan reflected, not to sneak into rooms: 'Open the door wide, *so*, come in through the centre of the doorway and face at once *towards* the patient, close the door quietly behind you and advance, making a cheerful remark.'

'Well? How are we?' the nurse had said, and paused in the middle of the room as if offering herself only as a momentary spectacle.

'Quite happy for the present. Are you going to stay with me for a bit?'

'I can't,' she said, 'I've got to attend to number eight,' and perceived the tray and came forward to take it. 'You've got to sleep now, till I come for you at five.' This, then, was farewell to humanity on this side of the barrier. Fan asked leave to smoke – a single cigarette. While giving permission the nurse got herself to the door and away, as if hurriedly, as if driven, and in a moment Fan heard her voice asking cheerful questions in the next room. The replies came in a moaning monotone.

There was chattering in an open doored room near by. Dining-room, common room of nurses on duty on this floor of the great house where they earned their livings amidst pain and death. Whirring of the lift. Footsteps. Gushing of water into a basin. Swift rinsing, more gushing of water.

The sounds brought vivid images that ought, she felt, to be shocking, and rousing her to resist their suggestive power. But they passed through her mind without attaining her. Between them and the centre of her attention was something that had been waiting within the quietude of the room for its moment. Approaching now, as she sat back against the raised

pillows and set down her book, with the note for Tom
sticking out of it like a book marker, on the table at her
side with cigarette case and matches. These doings
seemed the preliminaries to an interview.

A week ago, this moment of being left alone to wait
for the summons had drawn her forward into itself
and kept her there. She recalled the shock of finding
the life all about her no longer her concern, the cold
dry horror of the prospect of getting through the days
and playing her part. And how at times with an effort
she had forced herself out of her trance, dropped her
own cancelled life, and felt each life about her,
sharply, disinterestedly, seeing each one in its
singleness to be equally significant; been aware of a
strange, sure wisdom within her that seemed capable
of administering the affairs of everyone she knew,
guiding each life without offence. Had realised at one
moment with an overwhelming clarity how it is that
the character of an individual operates more
securely, upon those who have known him, after he is
dead. But for the last two days she had longed for this
moment and the relief it would bring.

It was like being in great open spaces, in solitude.
She rejoiced that she had decided not to tell Tom. This
strange, familiar intimation all about her owed the
power that was about to overwhelm her to her
undivided solitude. Agatha, going, had gone utterly. If
Tom had known, his suffering presence would have
been in the room with her. She was severed even from
Tom. With a deep, blissful sigh she felt all the ten-
sions of her life relax. She was back again in the
freedom of her own identity, in pre-marriage freedom, in more than childhood's freedom, with all the

strength of her maturity to savour its joy. In bright daylight the afternoon lay before her, endless – *the first holiday of her adult life* . . .

Laughing softly and luxuriously, beside herself with the joy of complete return, she looked gratefully about at the features of the ugly, barely furnished room and lit the permitted cigarette. The act of smoking threw her back to the minute before last. It was occupation, distraction, waste of priceless opportunity, of time. No, of something that was more than time! It was cutting her off from her deep life. It was unnecessary, because now she was back in her pre-smoking state of existence, and it had brought her to the present surface of life, away from the state of being into which she had just plunged. She crushed the burning end upon the match box. The edge of that first blissful expansion was blunted, but the fruit of its moments lay in her thoughts and in her refreshed, delighted limbs, and in her recognition of the way the hint of tobacco smoke upon the air enhanced the familiar, remembered, surrounding freshness that was like that of a dewy garden in the early morning. All about her, emanating from her relaxed mind, was all the garden and countryside beauty she had ever known, its concentrated essence, so that what she saw was not any single distinct scene, but a hovering and mingling of them all – their visible spirit which was one with her own.

If this blissful state were the gift of the holiday from responsibility and from the tension of human relationships that only the chance of death had had the power to give her, then perhaps the perfect certainty of death must always bring it at the last? Perhaps

people who were engaged in doing their dying were
enjoying, behind even the most awful of the outward
appearances, at the end of the exciting, absorbing
struggle that prevented them from communicating
their thoughts, the sense of being in its perfect
fullness . . .

She put down the book to question, as if it were a
person with her in the room, the fact that she had
forgotten, in the intensity of her absorption in *Green
Mansions*, what lay ahead. The experience had been
a fresh voyage of discovery into unchanged, under-
lying, timeless reality.

But with the book lying there closed, the sense of
passing time came back. Her watch said half-past
four. In half an hour . . .

The door opened upon the sister almost ostenta-
tiously displaying a hypodermic syringe. What hospital trick was this, sprung without warning?

'Your nurse is in the theatre, so I've come for this
little job.'

'What little job? What's the mystery in the syringe?'

'No mystery,' smiled the sister, slipping the jacket
from Fan's arm. 'We always give this before the
theatre.'

'Theatre, theatre, theatre,' absurd unsuitable
word for the reality now near at hand and to remain,
excluding all else for half an hour – an eternity –
after the sister had gone.

'It prevents bleeding,' said the steady, lying voice
below eyes that looked serenely through the window
as the syringe pricked home.

'I'd have gone quietly,' said Fan resentfully.

'I daresay you would. But now you'll be happy for a quarter of an hour before nurse comes.' She spoke sternly, but finished with a smile; . . . the gleeful smile of one who outwits a naughty child. Brush, between two women. Managers? All women are managers. That's why they daren't give in to each other. That's why . . . The nurse had gone. A quarter of an hour. Watch slow. This was some kind of drug. Stupefier. Very psychological. But that's why, I was saying . . . Thoughts would not come.

Her effort to call up a picture of the theatre brought only a confused sliding together of images in a mind that could not hold them. Oh, *very* psychological. Perhaps they were wise. She could not decide. Would have liked to go down in full possession of all her senses, yet was grateful for this not unpleasant numbness.

With the nurse at her side she was walking down a shallow flight of stairs. Towards death . . . life? At the bottom of the stairs was another nurse, who greeted her as she passed, and whose greeting she returned. A turning to the left, another nurse in the offing, standing like a sentry at an open door, who also said 'Good afternoon' and had to be answered.

This was the theatre. Not yet quite. A corridor leading to the theatre's arched doorway, but giving no vista. The nurse was behind now. She was going forward alone, quite clear-headed and very matter of fact, not needing this careful passing from hand to hand . . . In the doorway she was greeted by yet another nurse standing away to the right, leading her on with her dreadful 'Good afternoon.' Oh, *too* psychological. Farcical. She was round the bend.

Here it was, the lofty room, the white-clad forms, high windows open, no smell of anaesthetic or of disinfectant. Trees beyond the window.

Which still she could see as she lay – belonging, completing.

'Breathe quite naturally, Mrs Peele.'

Fresh and powerful came the volatile essences, playing in the air before her nostrils like a fountain. Her heart answered, her blood answered; but not herself. Desperately and quite independently her threatened heart fought against this power that was bearing her down. She raised her hands to still it.

'Clasp your hands.'

All of herself was in her clasped hands, beating, throbbing. Less, and less, and . . . less. . . .

HAVEN

PURLING awakes, as he had fully expected to do, within the deepest depths of peace. His eyes take in symmetrical oblongs of window curtain, densely patterned, yet transparent enough to admit, last night, the sky's faint glimmer and, this morning, golden light.

Urged out of bed by a sudden busy cheeping and scrabbling of sparrows, he feels beneath his feet the carpet's soft, clean surface and, in his mind, the dawn of a resolve: in this sequestered house, discovered by following his nose, and immediately announcing itself as his destination, he will remain aloof from his surroundings, keep the compass of his being firmly set, and thus achieve the concentration needed for the work in hand.

Ankle deep in his splash bath, he finds himself whistling with the liveliness of a guest hurrying to be breakfasting, amongst friends, in the glow of an overnight unity. Quelling the inappropriate mood born of the room's guest chamberly air, he recalls his expanded being to its centre.

'Shaving water. Breakfast in fifteen minutes.'

The woman's voice had reached him more directly through the closed door than when, face to face, he had asked his few questions and noted the toneless-ness of her replies. Yet even when slightly raised it revives his impression of her as a being serene and negative. The inevitable meeting and greeting will not dim, before he can use it, his morning clarity.

Clinkings, along the passage, of a carried trayful of crockery. Silence. The tinkle of a Swiss cowbell, muted, sweet. Her retreating footsteps. Breakfast is waiting. After breakfast he can hide, in here, while she clears, postpone meeting and conversation until later. The morning is safe.

Warm room. Fire cheerily burning. Savoury break-fast pleasantly set out. Stillness so perfect that he might be alone in the house.

His second cup of tea suggests that she may pre-sently appear to inquire if he would like more hot water. But she does not appear. He finishes his break-fast blissfully alone with the world in clear focus all about him, all he knows, all he has experienced, newly alive and available in virtue of this so blessedly unthreatened depth of concentration.

With the door wide open, he swings the little bell, sets it down upon the table, and retreats to his bed-room, shutting himself in with a soundfulness suffi-cient to reach the back premises. Hears Miss Tillard come down the passage and presently retire with her clinking trayful.

The odour of breakfast has gone, and the enervating, cosy glow surrounding him as he fed is replaced by a warm freshness. She has opened one of

the top lights and made up the fire. Upon the cleared
table stands the little bell. Her deputy. Unless
summoned she will not appear.

Mind and body abruptly failing, he relaxes in his
chair to emit, in comfort, a long sigh of relief. Like a
diver emerging from deep water with open eyes, he
becomes aware of the forgotten room and of its stillness, broken now by his movements as he gathers up
his scattered sheets, seeing, ahead, tomorrow and its
morning; an unnumbered series of tomorrows as good
as today.

Will it be possible? Is Miss Tillard, at last, the ideal
landlady? Will she, at the end of a fortnight, still be
remote? A fortnight; usually the outside limit. In all
his wanderings, sooner or later, gradually or suddenly, the current landlady's personality has flowed
in upon him, demanding attention like a presented
bill. Failure to honour the bill has bred an ever threat-
ening hostility. Destructive.

'Four conversaziones per day,' he groans in his
weakness. Even with Miss Tillard, featureless and
withholding as she seems to be, it will presently come
to that. Prison. Prison is the only complete refuge.
And perhaps even a gaoler, in the end, makes his
demands? She is gentle. Up to a point, cultured. It may
be possible to make rigorous terms. State, exactly,
the demands of one's work. But not until after lunch.
If now she were to enter the room, I should smile
myself, a happy convalescent, into her hands. Returning my inane smile, she would imagine that in her new
lodger she had found a friend, or a child.

Glancing at the clock, he sees that she may indeed

arrive at any moment now with the food he so eagerly
desires. Hurriedly he sweeps his belongings on to a
side table and decamps, again opening and shutting
doors with deliberate soundfulness.

In the shelter of his bedroom he looks out upon a
sunlit expanse. Unemotionally; seeing it merely as the
afternoon's exercise ground, and again sighs his happiness. For this absence of interest in an unknown
countryside is sure evidence of the favourable state.
An afternoon's restorative tramping, a little work
after a leisurely tea. No reading. Above all, no reading. After supper a meditative pipe or so, and then
early to bed with forces canalized for tomorrow.

When presently the little bell sounds its summons,
he seems to have heard it from that blessed sanctuary
a hundred times before, and turns serenely, fully
armed, towards lunch and landlady. Lunch indeed is
there, but Miss Tillard already has vanished.

After an excellent meal whose cold second course
had been set upon the table with the rest, he feels
almost eager to see and somehow to express grati-
tude. Placing a fireside chair so that he will be sitting
sideways to the rest of the room, he rings the bell and
sits down with his pipe, fully prepared for the inevitable interview. A gentle tap, and here she is.

Her serene 'Good afternoon' is less of a greeting
than a prelude to the further words which almost
drown his response. 'I want a list of the things you
don't like. Onions, for example,' and she reels off,
while busily clearing the table, a brief catalogue.
Assuring her of a catholic taste, he is about to become
complimentary when she begins again. 'Then I'll con-
tinue to prelude your breakfast with a cereal and

fruit, and sometimes there shall be fruit or a savoury
for lunch instead of a sweet. Anyhow, variety. At the
end of a week I'll consult you once more.' Leaving him
no time to respond, she hurries on: 'I'll give you tea at
half-past four, say toast and honey and a scrap of
homemade cake? And supper at nine?'

'That will suit me perfectly.' She is gathering up the
tablecloth. In a moment she will be gone. Now is the
time. But again her voice breaks in.

'I didn't suggest late dinner, which, of course, if you
prefer –'

Immediately voicing his disclaimer, he turns fully
round, to face her while expressing the amplitude of
his general appreciation, only to find, already
between them, the opened door.

'Principal meal at midday seems to fit country life.'
For the first time, her level voice, slightly raised
behind the sheltering door, has a ring of something
like vitality. 'And a latish supper shortens the evening.' Upon her last word, the door is gently closed.

For days he sees her no more. His dream is realised.
Here, at last, is indeed the perfect landlady. Better,
even, than the trained deaf mute for whom, again and
again, he has despairingly yearned. The whole of his
being is turned, untapped, upon his enterprise. Each
morning finds him ardently at work. Each afternoon
he flings himself into the open. Breathing the moistly
soft air of a mild January, he walks swiftly, heedless
of his surroundings, welcoming the early fall of darkness that is the herald of tomorrow. Daily, at some
moment on his tour, his eyes are called, his senses
challenged: by the last sun ray, madder rose upon a

crumbling gatepost, a leaf of hornbeam, burning out
its gold upon a stripped hedge. From such things he
turns swiftly away, feeling the joy they evoke flow
back into his being; restorative.

The third week brings cold. On its last morning a
dense grey sky is shedding hesitant flakes upon a
world grown white in a single night. The even, lurid
light banishes the sense of time. The further spaces of
the landscape have vanished behind a thick grey curtain. Perfection of enclosure. The writer's paradise.
As he rises from the breakfast table, Purling finds
himself drawn to the window. Flouting an inward
protest against any departure from the set pattern of
his daily movements, he goes down the room to pay,
within the spectral light of the window-space, a
moment's tribute to his benefactors. Exhilarated by
the chill given off by the panes and woodwork, he
stands bewitched, watching the eddying flakes
hover, as if of set purpose to beguile; each young flake
seeming aware of the magic effectiveness of its
irregular movement, the ecstatic quality of the sus-
pense created by its apparent hesitancy between
coming to rest upon earth and wavering upward to
hover once more amidst a ceaseless company. In a
moment desire rises within him, for another witness;
for someone to share and to reflect his exultation.

Here he stands, a truant, a boy caught by a spectacle, unable to escape. In vain he tells himself to
retreat as usual to his room across the passage. The
inner tumult, refusing to subside, turns him on his
heel. He tinkles the little bell and goes back to his post
at the window.

Stillness. Isolation with the muffled landscape and

the silent house. Away in her kitchen, before whose window the snow will be falling unnoticed, she listens, inanimate, for the closing of his bedroom door. Shall he ring again? Composedly she will advance down the passage to stand in the doorway, destroying, while she awaits a statement of his needs, the last remnant of his delight.

Escaping into memory, he finds Mother Shabley with him in the room, hurling into space as she lumbers about collecting his breakfast things, the outcries that will have rung through the house since dawn. Again he savours the relief he had known whenever exaggerated weather had supplied a topic for the inevitable morning interview. Once more he hears its daily accompaniment: the clatter announcing from upstairs the armed occupation of his bedroom. No refuge.

Here, all day long, is refuge; peace. Calling to him from the depths of this warm room, from the bracing chill of his empty bedroom across the passage. Cursing his moment's folly, he strides across to its shelter, closing its door with the usual signalling soundfulness, and strolls over to its window. The snowstorm is now in full swing. Large, mature flakes drive down, indifferently, thick and fast upon a busy errand that is no concern of his.

Restored to his fireside, he awaits, smoking a savourless pipe, the return of serenity. The room seems small, stuffy. Kept there by the absence of the vital stream usually flowing in through the top light, the odour of breakfast still hangs about. To banish preoccupation he paces to and fro, keeping his eyes downcast lest they betray him into investigating the still unfamiliar furniture. Turning for the third time from the welcome chill of the window space, he knows himself on the way back to his centre. Within his emptied consciousness is the stirring of desire to be at work. When he reaches the fireside he will collect and, in the character of servitor, lay out his materials. Then one more journey to the window and back. By that time his detachment will be complete. He is still a stranger, still nowhere and unknown. Mercifully, Miss Tillard is unaware of his escapade.

'Damnation! I'm still all over the place.' There it is, clear in his mind, placed there by a sudden treachery of the eyes: a complete picture of the room, its proportions, every detail of its furniture, a suite, one of identical millions.

Shocked by the bitter animosity within him, he makes for the fire, resolutely knocks out his half smoked pipe, pits against imagination's tumult the leisurely sounds of preparation for work and presently is seated, more or less serene, but unable any longer to draw inspiration from the very air of the unknown room. Wearily he sees ahead a daily battle for concentration amidst the contemptuous silence of the affronted furniture.

Pen in hand, he re-reads yesterday's pages and presently is drawing comfort from the swiftness of his discovery of what is wrong with a passage marked for revision. So it is to be one of those days, intermittent, usually produced by fatigue, when the reservoir is closed and one comes, as a stranger, to what it has so far produced. But this moment's reflection has left him with eyes half raised and set upon the near sideboard, noting its high polish, and in his mind a teasing statement stands like a placard: at intervals, perhaps every week, this room will be 'turned out'.

Returned to the faulty passage, he finds he has lost the phrase that a moment ago had leaped to the rescue. Fiercely he rounds upon the central enemy, his breakfast time emotion, unappeased and still manoeuvring. Mere languor, the normal occasional drop below form, allowing the critical to usurp the place of the creative faculty, he might profitably have used. But this emotional derailment is pure loss.

A fresh snowfall, shortening his walk, brings him home before teatime. The house seems alien. Its façade stares at him as if inquiring his business. For the first time he notices its weather-stains, the marks of its private experience. The door, sun-blistered, challenges his approach, seeming to warn him, as his hand reaches for the latch, that he will enter at his peril. Shall he turn back, brave the snowfall until oncoming darkness brings the promise of tomorrow?

The door opens upon immediate fulfilment of apprehension. Loud voices, laughter, echoing along the passage. Dominating the tumult, the voice of Miss Tillard, almost unrecognizable. Careless and gay, transforming the quiet interior.

While he stands listening, transfixed, the door, left open behind him for the shaking out of his snow-sprent coat, shuts with a resounding bang. Silence, abrupt and absolute. The kitchen door opens and Miss Tillard, flushed and dishevelled, comes hurriedly down the passage.

'What an afternoon! I'll make up your fire, and perhaps you'd like an early tea.'

His response, from the passage as she slides into

his room, a little eager and a pitch or two above his usual tone, sounds to him like a contribution to the recent din. Here he is, caught, entangled in society, playing a part.

When she returns with his tea, they discuss the weather, self-consciously expanding the topic, each waiting for the other to make an end.

Once more alone, Purling feels for a moment pleasantly social, relieved of the burden of his morning. But at a price that grows as he regards it, more and more appalling. His new world has fallen in ruins. For the moment, so long as she is engaged with her friends, the way lies open that leads to the point of departure for the space wherein for illimitable days he has dwelt with his vision. But only for the moment. Once her friends gone, and the two of them again alone in the house, the truth will settle down, perpetually vocal.

Continuously, henceforth, he will be aware of her: concentrated upon him and his needs, creeping about, muting, on his behalf, the sound of all her doings.

The alternative? To ask her, beg her, to go about her work and her recreation as if he were not there. She would understand. Certainly she is capable of that kind of understanding. Even so, with every sound in the house he would be aware of her, aware, worse still, of her awareness conscious of himself as its object; unable to achieve complete immersion.

Choice, between two kinds of invasion. Wreckage either way.

The surest security is in the lion's mouth? To be in the midst of an oblivious crowd. Part of it, unnoticed.

He recalls writers who have worked just anywhere. Dostoievsky, on a corner of the kitchen table, with the family clamorous all about him. Lawrence, tucked into any available space, and at once serenely oblivious. Peace at the heart of a storm. Storm comparable to that raging all the while at Mother Shabley's. Where, after all, he had done some of his best work. The life of the household, wrapped nourishingly about him, had yet left him untouched. *Had never come between him and himself.*

Excuse can easily be improvised. Will Mother Shabley's rooms be available? Where, amongst his still not unpacked belongings, are notepaper and envelopes?

SEEN FROM PARADISE

'JUST to let you know we are coming down on April 2nd. I can hardly believe it, though we've begun our terrific packing. Piles of books this time, besides all the rest. And we're bringing a tub plant, something Jim's brother knows all about and says blooms beautifully, to put at the side of the front door.'

Five days. Then events; crowding. Beginning with the setting down of the tub plant. Alien. Flouting the old grey cottage. Beginning of its gradual transformation. Each step of which, in turn, whenever I come down, I shall be expected to applaud.

All this I might have foreseen. But if ever I had looked ahead, even from one instant to the next, my winter would not have brought fulfilment of that autumn moment.

Soon after dinner. After dinner made late by my getting lost, gathering those mushrooms for London, on the cliff tops; drawn on and on by the gleaming circlets till misty twilight was there and night coming. Groping, I found at last the walled meadow; felt my way to its gate and the path towards the cliffside. Got somehow down, and home, triumphant. To find them distraught. Jim, I saw, could have shaken me for disturbing, by my alarming absence, the intensity of his evening vision of all he was leaving.

It was then, for the first time and by way of apology for his only partly jocular scolding, that he confessed *fear* of being out on the cliffs after dark and assured me the natives also felt afraid. Sunk in unaccountable happiness, I found no words. For a moment Jim was silent, reading my mood. Then, in the tone of one abandoning a hopeless case, he murmured into the tangle of twine engaging his hands: 'Don't forget you are in *Cornwall*.'

Cornwall. Cornwall. All through the spring, summer, autumn, he and I, whenever a region apart, we were outdoors by ourselves, had consciously shared the spell whose touch had first reached us when we got out on to the platform at the symbolically named St Erth.

Soon after dinner, the indoor evening enclosed us. Jim and Sylvia sitting collapsed, embodiments of departure, weary with packing. Nothing left to us of Cornwall but tomorrow's early grey, inaccessible in the bustle of getting off. Suddenly I knew I must be out again, alone, if only for a moment, in the Cornish night.

I got away unnoticed.

When my feet touched the mud of the lane, I felt again the timeless bliss sustaining me during my mushrooming on the cliff tops. As I went up the dark lane its power deepened. Suddenly brought me that thought of staying on alone in the cottage and sent me, to my own surprise, skipping into the air. All I then

knew was that the muddy roadway, the misty darkness, the voices of the sea, the melancholy beloved
hooting of the headland foghorn could be my own for
the endless deeps of winter.

When I went indoors with my plan, they were
incredulous. But presently Sylvia, though longing for
London and puzzled by my odd scheme, acclaimed, in
the deeps of her smile, the strange adventure, and
even Jim, while still producing objections, was privately aware of their uselessness. And when at last
he assured me that as far as they were concerned I
was more than welcome to the cottage, if only to keep
the place aired and dry, he was secretly giving,
emerged from surprise, a moment to envy of my coming solitude. And when at last he heaved himself up
from his chair to get on with the jobs still in hand, he
clearly revealed, by his deliberately averted glance,
his resentful awareness of my blissful longing for
their departure, from which longing, at that very
moment, I was distracted by the renewal of my sense
of the relative helplessness of men, of their dependence, however employed, upon all kinds of service,
matters that for them were mysteries without magic.
So that if he had turned to me instead of saying, by his
manner, so clearly that I could hear his very words:
'Well, so much for your interest in me and my work,'
he would have seen, not my pity, but a fellow feeling.
For to me, too, housekeeping was a repellent mystery.

The next morning, as soon as the sounds of their
departure had died away, I went, passing the open
door of the sound filled little room where we had
breakfasted, incredulously into the vacant sitting
room. Subsided into the nearest chair and sat drinking

in the stillness and discovering, bit by bit, the meaning of the moment in the lane. First, the all penetrating relief of knowing the world retreated to the immeasurable distance where, until the arrival of Sylvia's letter, it had remained. Then the surprise of discovering the disappearance of all desire to get out into the open. Until that moment I had never recognised, within the daily longing to wander amidst outdoor beauty, the powerful presence of the need to escape perpetual confrontation. From now on, the outdoor beauty would be all about me in the house, day and night, unobstructed.

Then a momentary panic. I remembered the tradespeople, Sylvia's daily palaverings at the front door. Each nothing less, in this leisurely countryside, than a social occasion. From all this Jim and I, absorbed in our writing, had been exempt. My winter was shattered. Until I remembered the blessedly roomy covered porch where, whenever we were going out for the day, Sylvia would leave messages. There, the postman could drop letters, the milkman his bottles, the village store its goods ordered by written list, the laundress her packages. Payments could confidently be left on the porch shelf. The yells of the swiftly perambulating fishmonger I would ignore. Beyond an occasional visit to the post office, in twilight, at teatime when there is nobody about, I need exchange no word with a living soul.

It must have been almost at once after this realisation of my security that I found myself gazing at my vanished world with a kind of affection I had never known before. Deep, inclusive. There they were, all my friends indistinguishable. Equally valuable and beloved, and as they began to fade, this strange new warmth moved on, across the world to its furthest inhabitants. My first voyage.

While still I was gazing, rejoicing in this newly revealed capacity of my own being, I saw, clear in the foreground, detached, and as if standing in space, the figures of just these two men. Incredibly together. My thoughts ran back across the years of friendship with each of them. Recalled my gradual gathering of their respective points of view. And their successive removal from my centre of interest.

On that morning I credited the selection of just those two to stand, clear of all the rest and restored to something of their original attractiveness, to the blissful expansion of my own being. And when I heard from Sylvia that indeed they had met and talked together, the psychic adventure of seeing them seemed less important than the revelation of my new relationship to all the world.

The memory of that morning, forgotten during my winter's work, comes back to me now because so soon I must be out in the world again? When once more I am in the midst of humanity, will that first morning's revelations fade away, or will they have given me the beginning of a new design for living?

Universal Ivory Tower?

Ivory Tower, the innermost sanctuary, sole reservoir for the tide ceaselessly flowing from beyond the spheres. Once this centre is reached, one's world is transformed. Will it remain transformed? At a price. The price of keeping the reservoir always available. That, not supplications, is the meaning of 'pray without ceasing'.

Universal ivory tower, the doorway to freedom? And to unity. Even for lovers? Even during the time while they believe themselves all-in-all to each other? For what then possesses them, in and through each other, and seeming to emanate from themselves alone, is what everyone is seeking? Cynics make game of this time, labelling it illusion. Wistful poets mourn its swift passing. But what *matters* is the illumination coming during this time of being in love. Even when the lovers are mistaken in each other and fall apart, the revelation remains, indestructible. Yes. This is true. And those who are together for life could retain consciousness of it if only, save in times of greeting and farewell, or upon special occasions when something urgent must be decided in haste, they would avoid confrontation, if only they would remain, as they were at the altar and at the wedding feast, side by side. They don't. Appalling, it is, to summon to mind the spectacle of all the married couples in the world sitting opposite each other; at table, at the fireside, each, for the other, obstructive, not only of the view, whether from window, or across a room, but also of thought wherein they may meet, or disagree, and, if disagreeing can do so far less destructively than when they clash in mutually visible opposition. On social occasions, too, the same mistake: sturdily supported by the ridiculous dogma of the impossibility of allowing husband and wife to be side by side.

Comically tragic it is to see, in a restaurant, a young couple out for an evening's enjoyment unconsciously destroying exactly what they came out to seek by sitting opposed, each, for the other summarising

dailiness. He, all too often, registering discomfort
while she, for the benefit of onlookers, keeps up a
would-be animated flow of talk designed to show that
all is well and the outing a success. Side by side, each
could relax and share a common spectacle, share,
too, the sense of togetherness that is at its strongest
when surrounded, *on neutral territory*, by fellow
creatures.

If I could get this truth about confrontation home
even to a few, especially to those serving life sentences, I should not have lived in vain. They would
pass it on to others.

Only five more days in solitude that not for one
instant has been loneliness. Fresh realisation, from
moment to moment, all the time. Everything available,
all past experience seen, while I sat writing, for the
first time as near, clear, permanent reality. An empty
mind as I sat in the evenings by the fireside doing
nothing, not needing to read or to think, just looking
and seeing, taking in afresh the marvellousness of
there being anything anywhere. Knowing, when I
went to bed, alone in the empty house that was
reported to be haunted, that I should sleep the night
through, dreamlessly, waking only when the early
light, gleaming through the small casements, gave me
again the joy of the squat jars of geranium-bloom,
brilliant against the pale canary yellow of the little
curtains. Summer in the wintry dawn.

Now, for the first time, I begin to be qualified to
meet the world? To share, even when surrounded,
exactly when surrounded, the rich deeps of solitude?

'Just to let you know we'll be coming down on the
2nd.' Five more days. Five whole days. But what is

this on the other side? 'Do you think you could per-
suade old George to let us have a small beer barrel for
the tub plant? An old one would do. If he had it ready,
we could pick it up as we pass in the wagonette.'

So this is the end, today, now, this minute. The
remaining days swept away by a preoccupation.

Damn the tub plant!

Yet even now, now that I have said farewell, I am
not disstressed. Something remains, has become a
part of me, for ever.

For ever with me is that meeting with old George.
There he stands, sunlit, in his doorway, a sturdy lifetime of experience, listening to my plea with eyes
withdrawn, after the first moment, upon reality; the
cautious, meditative gaze that townspeople so easily
mistake for bucolic slowness in the uptake. Rich, and
nourishing, when George had heard the whole of my
appeal, came his gently protesting discourse,
addressed to the universe, upon the subject of barls,
precious reservoirs growing with age ever richer and
more enriching.

'Aw, naw, me-dear, they barls don't belong to be
scatted.'

Inspired, in the midst of my disappointment, by the
possession of a small region of knowledge, happy in
the sense of having made my return journey into the
world hand in hand with this gentle old wiseacre, I
went gladly on to the village shop to acquire one o'
they little barls they use for lard and such. Whenever
I behold the plant set in its crudely smooth enclosure I
shall substitute, in imagination, one of old George's
sacred reservoirs.

EXCURSION

ON yet another evening, their voices, gathered together. One voice, in variations.

'You're not too near the window, Gran?'

'No; thanks, dear. The wind seems to have dropped.'

'This one usually does towards the end of the day.' Yes. Leaving a splendid sky: huge clouds piled along the horizon, lit by sunset; then by afterglow slowly fading. Jane loves it just as I do. Jane knows all about the doings of the winds.

'Thank God for *that*. This coast's *all* wind. That filthy one last night kept me awake for hours. By the way it must be nearly blackout. Anybody got the time?'

'Don't worry, Daph. In any case we'll see the lights vanish across the way when they do theirs.'

Jane wants to keep the sky as long as possible. But she won't say so. Neither would I. To mention it may, or may not, pass it on to someone who has not yet observed; but spoils it a little for oneself.

'No lights there. I can see the windows. Besides, even if there *were*, they might be watching for *ours* to go up when we blackout. They're either out or gone. I believe they're gone.'

'Poor Daph. You've been hoping that for days.'

'Well Jane, who hasn't? You know *perfectly* well you've been every bit as fed up with that indescribable kid raising hell all day long. Besides, you've only to *think*. All the schools have to start before Friday. And this morning there was a car. I heard it. All their voices shouting down the engine.'

'And you didn't prance out and yell to the shover to stop that infernal row?'

'Don't be silly. This hole isn't *town*. And it wasn't two in the morning. Besides, I never said infernal.'

'No. She said *blasted*. Don't contradict me. Hear my fact. Decisive. A coal-cart. Yesterday afternoon.'

'Peter! Why on earth didn't you tell us? That settles it. They've *let. All* the swear words!'

'Oh, well, Daph, it mayn't be so bad. Perhaps just those ghosts who were there last term. Living in the kitchen we hardly knew they were there.'

'Wishful thinking. And anyway it makes no difference to you, with your window at the back. They don't overlook *you* and make you get up with stuffy curtains drawn and the lights on. Foul.'

'Perhaps there's no one. Anyway we'll soon know.'

'Anyway we've got to *blackout*. We may as well do it now and have done with it.'

'Aow!'

'Well, Jane, you *know* what it'll be if we're late. Do you *want* the natives banging at the door?'

'We won't forget. Anyway, even down here, the wardens nowadays ain't so pertikler to a few minutes.'

'Carried, with amendment. Police, not wardens.
Meantime what about a light?'

'Yes, precious. Switch it on. You've been a lamb,
Peter. Have you been cursing me?'

'Oooh-noo. Been taking in your sky-show. Extra
special show.'

A knife, turning in one's heart. This sky will be a
part of his embarkation leave. To be remembered in
God *knows* what circumstances. Its light is nearly
gone. The light that hides the stars. Our light is on, our
little indoor sun. Jane loves them both. So, I believe,
does Peter. He'll now produce the book that is too big
to take back to camp. Jane will keep on knitting, with
an eye on the sky till blackout. I shall have to move,
then, away from my little retreat, my sky lit window
seat, back again towards tomorrow.

'Now that we can see, let me tell you, Daph, on the
authority of my newly-mended watch, that the time is
. . . twelve and a quarter minutes past seven . . . the
next part of the programme follows . . . in . . . just
under three minutes. Nearly the whole of which the
good man wastes in haltingly specifying the record he
proposes to put on. Don't worry. I'll keep an eye.'

'There's a female announcer who, if there's a gap,
doesn't waste a second, puts on a jolly march.'

Black and tan collie. Hurling himself, all alone, along
the empty esplanade. Leaping. Barking as he leaps.
Wild with joy. His barks go up into the sky, making me
look up and realise how high it is. Up and up and up.
For the first time. I didn't know. Now I know. I've seen
it, and I know, and shall never, never forget. Up and
up and up and up. But looking again is not quite the

same as the first look. It is that I shall remember,
always. A secret. People will come, later on, after
breakfast. But they won't see the sky as it is when it's
alone, when there's nobody about and nothing going
on.

We must have gone to bed, we youngsters, the night
before, forlorn, with seaside at an end and nothing
ahead but the early morning train at the forgotten
railway station up at the back of the town. We shall
have been up betimes. Neatly dressed for the journey.
Stockings covering sunburnt legs. Mary's hair in a
bun. Ellen's a doorknocker. Pug and I in pigtails.
Gloves. The luggage in the passage. And then, the
letter for Mary. 'Children!' I hear her excited voice.
'Another week! Mother says we can stay another
week!' I must have rushed out, just before breakfast,
unable to bear, indoors, the overwhelming joy. In a
fraction of a second, all darkness gone. All menace.
No railway station, its clangour enhanced by the certainty of missing the train, by the dread of a sudden
loud shriek from some near engine. No long moments
of cowering in the carriage with my fingers in my ears
until our own engine should have shrieked. Instead,
the impossible restoration of every joy. Endless per-
spectives. Today not yet begun. Not to begin until
after breakfast. Then Sunday, an interim, rich, as it
drew to its close, with anticipation of the week ahead,
and bringing, at the seaside, its own negative joys: no
visit to Grannie, no desperate search, after the first
greetings, for something to say to her that must be
shouted, several times, down her long speaking tube,
only to hear, when at last she had caught one's words,
her querulous, disconcerting, 'Is that *all*?' No

children's service, all humiliation, and the embarrassment of singing, without a choir, *We are but little
children weak*. Grown-up church instead, everyone
looking seasidey despite Sunday clothes, and every
moment of the long day bringing nearer the days
stretching away ahead further than one can see.
Each with a morning, afternoon, evening. Bringing
successive joys. Climbing the wooden steps of the
bathing machine, away out of the bright sunshine into
the dark, damp interior, keeping one's balance as the
machine hurtles, to the jerky unwinding of its cable,
unsteadily over the sands towards the sea; hurried
disrobing and getting into the clumsy two-piece bathing dress; opening the back door on the sudden
glinting expanse of sunlit water; forgetfulness of
everything in the shock of the cloudy salt water; loss
even of one's own identity in swimming, tadpoling
about until called to climb up the steps, plunge back
into darkness and peel off one's heavy sodden gown
in the damp, cold partition just inside the door. Paddling, breaking up with one's toes the lovely network
of gold in the sunlit shallows. Shrimping in rock pools;
glad and sorry when the draining away of sand
reveals the little wriggling forms leaping in the net
and, here and there, a large, whiskered prawn. Donkey rides, the warm smell of leather and donkey skin.
Sitting on the sand round the nigger minstrels,
growing more and more blissful as each well-known
item faithfully returns, and hungry and hungrier as
the morning draws to a close. Fruit pie and cream
every day for the second course. More paddling and
shrimping in the afternoon, after the short rest that
brings, instead of sleep, blissful listening to the

outdoor sounds. And in the evening, when at home the day would be over, going out on to the lamplit esplanade below which the faithful sea flumps or whispers in the darkness, to hear Pat Murphy sing his songs standing up in his cart beside the cottage piano: *Father O'Flynn, The Yeoman's Wedding, Fiddler and I, Off to Philadelphy, Enniscorthy, Ballyhooley.* Singing refrains, with the rest of the crowd, at the tops of our voices. Singing words, regardless of their meaning, to lilting music:

'Willaloo-oo-oo, and we'll *all* enlist ye know,
  For the principles and illiments they cha-arm me,
For they don't care what they *ate*, if they get their whisky *nate*,
  In the Ballyhooley Blue-ribbon Arrr-my.'

All these things will have crowded upon me, standing together in my enraptured mind. And then the dog barked, and I forgot them. And now, after sixty years and more, whenever Weymouth is recalled to me it is not the seaside joys that return, but that first discovery of the sky. And each time more vividly than before. Just now, I felt the shock of it pass through me like an electric current. It is not memory.

Strange that only tonight the muffled bark of that dog across the way should restore this experience. Often I heard him when those folks were there before. And constantly down here one hears the sudden abrupt bark of a collie: that great fellow at the farm, when he is collecting the cows. Several round about the Bay, when they chase gulls, or just let off joy in capering about untrammelled by roads. 'Association of ideas' describes the process without accounting for it. Certain conditions, certain states of being, especially favour reentry into what we call 'past moments'? But they are not past.

'Our three and a half minutes nearly *hup*, Daph.'

Peter's voice, Peter's words shutting down upon incommunicable experience. Shutting down, too, upon his own incommunicable experience.

'They're there,' she said, and saw Jane's bent head swiftly rise, and read, in the investigating glance that preceded her smile, an anxious question: has Grannie begun to wander?

One of these days, perhaps before long, as I sit listening to the talk of others, a chance phrase, or some sudden evocative sound, will so deeply involve me in experience that I shall be unaware of speaking from the midst of it, irrelevantly, into a current occasion. Perhaps, even worse, I shall produce the sound known as a senile giggle. Shocked, they will be. Jane, solicitous. Needlessly. Not knowing that it is the old who find, and that almost ceaselessly, cause for solicitude: for shell-bound youth. It holds me for these three. Less for Jane, who, from babyhood, has had intimations. Peter, too, up to a point. But his perceptions are apt to be specialised, restricted, comedic. Daphne's excited angers measure her awareness of wealth available. And prevent the acquisition of even a farthing. Both Jane and Peter will know, when their great moments come, the worse than uselessness of trying to hold them. Yet already they have mourned, as in my own time I mourned, over the passing of a scene, a mood, a set of circumstances. Unable to recognise these as their possessions, immortal, inexhaustible. Unable to discover their wealth until they are old and 'wandering in their minds'. Life makes artists of us all? No longer seeing experience chronologically, we can compose it, after the manner of a picture, with all the parts in true prespective and relationship. Moving picture. For moments open out, reveal fresh contents every time we go back into them, grouping and regrouping themselves as we advance.

Smiling, she was aware of Jane, gathering up the smile, adding it to the sudden worlds, speculating.

'Those folks *are* there again,' she said briskly, raising her voice against Daphne's impatient swishing of the blackout curtains: 'the ones who were there before.'

'Gran, dear, how *do* you know?'

'Their dog; just now; I heard it; inside the house.'

'That settles it. Damn.'

'Well, Daph, we oughtn't to expect *any* house down here to stand empty nowadays.'

'For heaven's sake tell me something I *don't* know!'

And now the dog was barking in the open. Enthusiastically. Being taken for his evening run. Another evening moving towards its temporary end. Moving into store.

DEATH

THIS was death this time, no mistake. Her cheeks flushed at the indecency of being seen, dying and then dead. If only she could get it over and lay herself out decent before anyone came in to see and meddle. Mrs Gworsh winning, left out there in the easy world, coming in to see her dead and lay her out and talk about her . . . While there's life. Perhaps she wasn't dying. Only afraid. People can be so mighty bad and get better. But no. Not after that feeling rolling up within, telling her in words, her whom it knew, that this time she was going to be overwhelmed. That was the beginning, the warning and the certainty. To be more and more next time, any minute, increasing till her life flowed out for all to see. Her heart thumped. The rush of life beating against the walls of her body, making her head spin, numbed the pain and brought a mist before her eyes. Death. What she'd always feared so shocking, and put away. But no one knows what it is, how awful beyond everything till they're in for it. Nobody knows death in this rush of life in all your parts.

The mist cleared. Her face was damp. The spinning in her head had ceased. She drew a careful breath. Without pain. Some of the pain had driven through her without feeling. But she was heavier. It wasn't gone either. Only waiting. She saw the doctor on his way. Scorn twisted her lips against her empty gums. Scores of times she'd waited on him. Felt him drive fear away. Joked. This time he'd say nothing. Watch, for her secret life to come up and out. When his turn came he'd know what it was like letting your life out; and all of them out there. No good telling. You can't know till you're in for it. They're all in for it, rich and poor alike. No help. The great enormous creature driving your innards up, what nobody knows. What you don't know . . . Life ain't worth death.

It's got to be stuck, shame or no . . . but how do you do it?

She lay still and listened for footsteps. They knew next door by now. That piece would never milk Snowdrop dry. Less cream, less butter. Everything going back. Slip-slop, go as you please, and never done. Where'd us be to now if I hadn't? That's it. What they don't think of. Slip slop. Grinning and singing enough to turn the milk. I've got a tongue. I know it. You've got to keep on and keep on at them. Or nothing done. I been young, but never them silly ways. Snowdrop'll go back; for certain . . .

But I shan't ever *see* it no more . . . the thought flew lifting through her mind. See no more. Work no more. Worry no more. Then what had been the good of it? Why had she gone on year in year out since Tom died and she began ailing, tramping all weathers up to the field, toiling and aching, and black as thunder most times. What was the good? Nobody knew her. Tom never had. And now there was only that piece downstairs, and what she did didn't matter any more. Except to herself, and she'd go on being slipslop; not knowing she was in for death that makes it all one whatever you do. Good and bad they're all dying and don't know it's the most they've got to do.

Her mind looked back up and down her life. Tom. What a fool she'd been to think him any different. Then when he died she'd thought him the same as at first, and cried because she'd let it all slip in the worries. Little Joe. Tearing her open, then snuggled in her arms, sucking. And all outside bright and peaceful; better than the beginning with Tom. But they'd all stop if they knew where it led. Joe, and his wife, and his little ones, in for all of it, getting the hard of it now, and death waiting for them. She could tell them all now what it was like, all of them, the squire, all the same. All going the same way, rich and poor.

The Bible was right, remember now thy Creator in the days of thy youth. What she had always wanted. She had always wanted to be good. Now it was too late. Nothing mattering, having it all lifted away, made the inside of you come back as it was at the first, ready to begin. Too late. Shocking she had thought it when parson said prepare for death, live as if you were going to die tonight. But it's true. If every moment was your last on earth you could be yourself. You'd dare. Everybody would dare. People is themselves when they are children, and not again till they know they are dying. But conscience knows all the time. I've a heavy bill for all my tempers. God forgive me. But why should He? He was having his turn anyhow, with all this dying to do. Death must be got through as life had been, just somehow. But how?

When the doctor had gone she knew she was left to do it alone. While there is life there is hope. But the life in her was too much smaller than the great weight and pain. He made her easier, numb. Trying to think and not thinking. Everything unreal. The piece coming up and downstairs like something in another world. Perhaps God would let her go easy. Then it was all over? Just fading to nothing with everything still to do . . .

The struggle came unexpectedly. She heard her cries, and then the world leapt upon her and grappled, and even in the midst of the agony of pain was the surprise of her immense strength. The strength that struggled against the huge stifling, the body that leapt and twisted against the heavy darkness, a shape with her shape, that she had not known. Her unknown self rushing forward through all her limbs to fight. Leaping out and curving in a great sweep away from where she lay to the open sill, yet pinned back, unwrenchable from the bed. Back and back she slid, down a long tunnel at terrific speed, cool, her brow cool and wet, with wind blowing upon it. Darkness in front. Back and back into her own young body, alone. In front of the darkness came the garden, the old garden in April, the crab-apple blossom, all as it was before she began, but brighter . . .

AUTOBIOGRAPHICAL SKETCHES

BEGINNINGS

A BRIEF SKETCH

BEING born in Berkshire should mean early acquaintance with woods and hills and rivers. It meant these things for me. Long before their names were known to me they had given that first direct knowledge which instruction and experience can amplify and deepen, but can never outdo. I had noted the play of light through a wood and the astonishing presence of flowers and ferns upon its floor where open spaces were clear of undergrowth – guests, like myself, of the giant trees and the light and the vast quietude; had visited a hilltop and discovered that the world went on beyond it; had noted along the river bank, the strange independent plants that knew neither home nor kindness, and the flow of that river, on and on, away, homeless and free.

Berkshire was also a vast garden, flowers, bees and sunlight, a three-in-one, at once enchantment and a benevolent conspiracy of awareness turned towards a small being to whom they first, and they alone, brought the sense of existing. Alternating with South Devon, sea, rock-pools, cowries sea wet and heavy in the hand with an infinite preciousness; gift of the sea that extended outwards forever and had no further shore. Just as a window in an Oxford chapel, I believe Oriel, seen when I was six years old, extended within itself forever, so that at once one escaped those who mysteriously had brought one to this opening into reality and proceeded alone, on and on, into that window, knowing it had no end.

Berkshire, of course, was many other things, including home and its inhabitants and a thousand inexhaustibles, many of them named. But it was these other, nameless things that then made the stronger impression. And it was because the sudden sweeping away of them all, soon after Oriel window, made way, at least for another sea, that heartbreak was presently healed. A Sussex sea, a populous town. Strangers impinging, the sense of a vast company of people by no means all of one mind. The dawning, amazing realization of illiberality, in thought and feeling, hitherto unappreciatedly absent amongst the adults inhabiting my home. And in exchange for the first little school attended between my fifth and sixth years and merely enormously increasing the number of inexhaustibles, and revealing 'people' as fellow guests in wonderland (either unaware of their state and therefore hateful, or aware and therefore themselves inexhaustible and comfortably not to be troubled about) another school. Competition, dimly sensed, and rivalry, and their destructiveness. Boys, envisaged collectively, negatively objectionable. One fell in love, from a distance, with a nose, a pair of

eyes, the chinline, seen in profile, of some unknown
god, young, but nearer to omniscience and omni-
potence than, by this time, one could admit his elders
ever to be. Yet there was a shadow of uncertainty.
For the sound of a voice, heard by chance, would
either hurl a god from his throne or cure, for a while,
life's most incurable ills.

My eighth year brought London, in the form of a
spacious suburban house whose garden restored a
lost eternity. Tennis, boating, dancing. School, meaning only languages, music, drilling, and song and,
always haunted by the shadow of misgiving, the fascination of 'the wonders of science'. School competed
even with holidays, competed, almost successfully,
with other worlds, for ten years. Leaving was heartbreak, discovered as the heartbreak of losing chosen
friends. From this pain, only the writing of words,
preferably rhymed, could bring relief.

So far plain sailing. But what, in a brief sketch, may
be said of any of our lives from seventeen onwards?
Bare skeleton of facts. Ceaseless conflict of adolescence, the harsher for the sudden removal of all
props. Isolation, going forth into the world unarmed,
to make a living unprepared. Teaching, abroad, at
home, in school and in family. Each a brief and
fascinating and horrible experience. Strange poses
of an untrained dancer. At last, London, clerical
work, 'freedom'. The Quest. Love, all sorts, art, all
sorts, religion, all sorts, all saying in chorus, 'Lo here,
and Lo there.' But is not all this experience written in
a million volumes by a million writers? Thought,
about everything. The beginnings of the divided mind.
Recognition of the universality of the alternative

interpretation. Of the difference between knowledge and knowing, confirmed by the voice of experience when it turns with a grin and says 'I told you so'; and so forth, for years, until the not uncommon desire to focus from a distance takes one away from 'everything and everybody'. And once again and the more powerfully for the intervention of instruction and of experience, one rediscovers what was known before these began their work of befogging and destruction. And one begins in 1908 to write, having already served one's apprenticeship in the pages of a vivid, if obscure, anarchist monthly. And what one writes is welcomed by the kindly editor of the *Saturday Review*.

And one hovers between London and the country, feeling each enhanced by the process. And discovers Cornwall and makes it the land of one's adoption. And the war finds one with the first chapter written of a long, long book, and the second begun, and the third in shape; one is therefore, when the time comes, incensed in being classified as a post-war writer altogether.

A FEW FACTS FOR YOU...

Constantine Bay, Padstow, N. Cornwall

Dec. 34

Dear Sylvia Beach,

A few facts for you to select from, for I assume your note will be of the briefest.

The sudden collapse of a happy home, life in ample surroundings flung D. R. on the world at the age of seventeen without qualifications for the art of making a living. A few years of teaching, in private schools and in a family, was followed by clerical work in London (£1.0.0 per week). Before overwork, including the joining of various societies, political and other, and the explorations of all the 'isms', and the writing of contributions to various eccentric magazines, brought breakdown, she had planned a book on the inviolability of feminine solitude or, alternatively, loneliness.

In 1908–10, escaped from London, she contributed a series of sketches to the *Saturday Review* and, at intervals, to various dailies. *Pilgrimage* was mapped out in 1909, in a summer house on a fruit farm. After years of hackwork and translation, the (first) chapter, *Pointed Roofs*, was written in 1913 and published in 1915. Since then nine further chapters have appeared, the last, *Dawn's Left Hand,* in ——. A further chapter is in preparation.

In regard to bibliography, I fear I cannot be very helpful. I receive many press-cuttings about books on the novel wherein my work is dealt with, but have read none of them save the Chevalley's *le Roman de nos jours*. Articles innumerable there have been. I have read few and kept none. An interesting point for the critic who finds common qualities in the work of Proust, James Joyce, Virginia Woolf and D. R. is the fact that they were all using the 'new method' though very differently, simultaneously.

Proust's first volume appeared in 1913 while D.R. was finishing *Pointed Roofs*. She preceded J.J. and V.W. but they were writing their books when hers appeared.

Alan suggested a few of his collection of cuttings in regard to the last published volume of P. (And wants them returned.)

I am very sorry I can't be more helpful.

Yours sincerely

DOROTHY M. RICHARDSON

WHAT'S IN A NAME?

WHAT'S in a name? – Feeling that knowledge of the facts leading to his canonisation
might exorcise the lingering vestiges of the spell he
cast over my childhood, I passed many years
intending one day to seek out the story of Botolph.
And though I have never made my pilgrimage to the
fount of fact, I still hope that one day on some quiet
page this saint will flower for me into reality. But I
doubt whether even when I possess the record that
earned him the dedication of a church, the burden of
his name will be quite lifted from my spirit.

Meanwhile I suspect, I hope, that he has not many
churches. I suspect that the builder of the church that
laid waste two years of my childhood's Sundays was
trying, when he named it, for something uncommon. I
may wrong him. He may have loved Botolph. May
even have felt the misfortune of his name, its lonely
ugliness amongst the saintly names, and have offered
him therefore with a special tenderness a stately
church. For the church, as I remember it, is stately: in
size. All else, save the smell meeting one at its open

door, I have forgotten. And my other churches, the one preceding and the one following the church of Botolph, I remember well.

St Botolph's is the void, flatulent of horror, that prepared my small mind for the agnosticism assailing it two years later in the church I loved best and from whose sheltering grace my childish repudiations could not, even for a single Sunday, keep me away.

It was St Botolph's, though at the age of six I could not bodily absent myself, that saw my first spiritual desertion. St Botolph's that first separated church from home. And though there must be, a scattered band, souls homing in memory to Botolph's church, the unhappy choice of its founder has robbed them of much. For there is in his name neither shelter nor fragrance. There is no breath of any kind of beauty in the word that in English touches the mind like the edge of an inflated balloon. Botolph no doubt earned and should have his churches. But not in England.

There are certain names that fit English churches. The straightforward and, for the ear alone, uninspiring SS. John, James, George, Martin, and Mary. These names can be all things to all men. But *Botolph* . . .

Then there are the subtle names that have increased with the growth of Anglicanism: Olave, Magdalen, Cecilia, Jude. Very many of them the names of women. Churches emanating from the Catholic spirit that while it excludes woman from the ultimate sanctities of the church on earth is yet constrained to set her above, crowned; Queen of heaven. And it is to a woman that my first church was dedicated. My first church, hear its sweet sound, was St

Helen's. St Helen's – gentle interior, living in my
memory as soft bright colour broken upon carved
stone and wood, continuous colour upon rooted form,
in every direction an eyeful of beauty – I have never
left. There was another church, an alternative, the
church I was taken to in the rain. It, too, was an abode
of beauty, but sterner, less coloured, less warmly
welcoming, and dedicated to Martin. The Martin who
gave his cloak. But Martin never enfolded me as did
the gentle Helen.

St Helen's was my mother church and wraps my
spirit still, though the love of my earliest indepen-
dence was to be given to the church, plain brick, and
sparsely decorated, that first gave me music. There
was a long journey to a new home, and almost my first
memory of the new home is of hearing the opulent
name of the new church: All Saints, and of imagining
its upper air filled with winged figures. My first visit
found its cool sternness veiled by the flowers of Easter
and their scents. And always it was veiled by the music
of its services, music, ruled by a master and confined
to the work of masters, that caught and for years
trained and disciplined my young senses unawares.

There was a shock, following hard on the heels of
that first revelation and dimming for a while the joy of
my escape from Botolph. I learned that the new secret
home was a Chapel of Ease to the Church of St John.
Disquieting mystery. I saw John afar off, difficult and
stern, and my crowd of winged saints easy and
indulgent. Ease there was. I knew that at once. Ease
for my two years' soreness of spirit. But John's
church challenged and beckoned. Until I was taken
there and found it musty, too large to be filled with the
scents of no matter how many flowers; dark without

being mysterious, and harsh without austerity. I refused a second visit and no longer minded that my church was called a chapel.

And when my final rebellion came, when my young mind rose up and smote the creeds, it was the creeds imagined as recited in the churches of Botolph and of John that I repudiated. Still faithful to All Saints I gave up taking my mind there and felt as my senses feasted, a dawning nostalgia.

But it was at Botolph's hated door that my mind had first drawn back. I remember the moment, the loneliness of that first assertion. There was, leading to the church, a straight road, treeless. Long it probably was not. But I remember it as interminable. At intervals there were houses, large brick houses soured by being heralds of the final bitterness of St Botolph's, and surrounded by high walls that allowed no glimpse of gardens. My spirits, flagging always on leaving the winding ways of the old town for this bleak stretch of road, one day failed utterly, and I wept my despair aloud. That my spirits would be high and my pace eager if at the end of my walk there waited something that I loved, was the burden of the rebukes administered by outraged elders. That was true. Too true. But my logic had no words. And for words if I had had them, my bitterness was too deep.

What actually did wait at the end of the dreary road, what was the quality of the food offered to youth and age in the hated edifice, I shall never know. But I know that always, treading that *via dolorosa*, I heard the sound: *Botolph*. I heard it in the porch, where the flat damp smell came forth to slay the outer air. I identified it with the figure of the corpulent verger. A church by *any* other name . . .

*J*OURNEY TO PARADISE

W HEN we are lords at last of earth and sea and the spell of the wild shall have retreated to the stars, the charm of coasts will remain, the ancient charm of land and sea in relationship. It is a thing inexorable even by villas, even in a world imagined as edged along the whole of its coastlines by promenades, villa-fringed. And indeed, wild coast, now so rapidly diminishing, was, for the majority, until the present century, until the coming of motors, even in England almost unknown. There was the ocean, across which brave people ventured for diversion or for business. And there was the seaside, certain known strands, frequented in the proper season. The interspaces were legendary, matter for travellers' tales. And a visit to even the best known and most easily accessible resort was an enterprise fraught with so many perils that every book of household management offered a little homily on the subject of sea air – a substance only less redoubtable than night air – and a discourse on the dangers of bathing. To the end of my days, though I have shed more of this lore than I can recall, I shall know just how long one should acclimatise before venturing into the water, how long to remain therein, the best restoratives to take on mergence, and the number of minutes that may safely be spent in resting before the sharp walk that is essential to survival from the ordeal.

From our earliest years my sister and I were familiar with every detail of the ritual, discussed, no doubt, each summer in advance by our parents and nurses, and serving, I fancy, with them no less than with ourselves only as an enhancement of the coming adventure. It is certain that once we had arrived they were immediately forgotten. Bathing, which began on the first morning, I remember as an exciting and tiresome interruption of entrancements, of building and dyke making, shell gathering, shrimping, wading or mere ecstatic pattering about to the movement of sea and sky and cliffs. It was exciting because that quaint Quaker invention, the bathing machine, rattled across the sands at a tremendous pace, and it was happiness, while being unrobed, to stand on the bench in the dark enclosure and watch through the tiny square of window the outside brilliance racing by. Bathing was tiresome because the hands of the huge bathing women who stood about in the shallows and cut short private enterprise by dipping us one by one turn and turn about beneath the advancing waves were large and red and very hard. The interruption over we immediately followed our own devices, though I remember that there were, if no restoratives, at least buns, incomparable brown sun-hot new buns, to allay the worst pangs of a most ferocious hunger.

To this day when in London I prepare for a swift rush to the coast I know that I am going, not casually to the sea, but marvellously to the seaside; the seaside that is one place and has no name. The place that was seaside to me in my childhood, being in South Devon, had a rich and lovely name, a name that my father, with a touch of jocular patronage, used to speak in the West Country fashion, and my childish condemnation of his pose was in reality a resentment of any naming of my heaven. I know now how unjust I was, that the young man, ancient to me, who doughtily, summer after summer, carried his offspring the long day's journey to the far west, took refuge in the local speech because he, too, was shy of naming the unnameable. He, too, was going to the seaside. And I can appreciate, knowing that although seaside is one and indescribable, there are shores and shores, the excellence of his choice. For though today I love the pale and narrow sea that tumbles heavily upon the Sussex coast, the fresh little sea dancing in the east wind off Norfolk, the green Atlantic rollers that break against the Cornish cliffs, and many another stretch of our island waters, each one brings between-whiles the nostalgia of my own seaside, of the fine, fine shingles of the Devon beaches, the recurrent sound of them under the tide, the infinitely refreshing hiss and wash as they are lifted and dragged backwards by the waves, and the echoes of this sound in the red caves and tunnels. For years I knew no other coast. Did not know that there were cliffless beaches of grey pebble, pallid in unbroken sunlight, and waves that retired soundlessly over sands of muddy grey. The first sight of such pebbles and such sands seemed heartbreak.

And I have seen Devon triumph, seen her coast a lifetime of other coasts.

My seaside is no longer the seaside that I knew. But the pier and promenade that have usurped the places of the old stone jetty and the sea wall have not changed the sound of the sea in the coves nor dimmed the beauty of the innumerable shells washed up there. A handful of shingle still yields cowries, the small tooled shapes that were nuggets in dross to my eager hands, minutely heavy, sea wet and pinky brown in their fine ribbings along the spine, paling to where the lips curl inwards, ivory white.

But it was not of these things that I thought when into endless summer, into a garden whose boundaries were as yet unknown, there came the news of the great journey, but rather of the dazzling spaces of sunlit salty air above the little town and of the way sound echoed through it fresh and free. Morning sounds, the blithe barking of a dog upon the shore, the shrill high voice of the fishwife announcing my incomparable seaside breakfast, and later the sounds of donkeys trotting and of people hurrying to the beach on silent rubbered feet to laughter and the clinking of little buckets. The air above the small town behind the cliffs held always some echoes, and this for me was its deepest charm, haunting me while I conned over with my sisters the joys to come. Nothing could fully banish its enchantment, neither the childish squabblings that at home could fill the universe with darkness, nor the first misery of scorched legs nor even the recurrent tragedy of bedtime. And though each day I was lost in the joy of the strong red cliffs, the happy wash and ripple of the waves, the shapes and colours of the lovely things to be seen and handled in rock pools, my best bliss came down upon me away from the shore. All that made seaside was fused and distilled within the dazzling air above the open space where our house stood in the mainway of the townlet, a wide road divided by narrow ribbons of green lawn that ran each side of a stone-rimmed torrent broken every few yards by a steeply gushing fall. I felt both pity and contempt for these tame sweet waters. Yet it was in passing over the little bridge that spanned their gentle rush to the sea, in hearing the plash and murmur of their cascades go up into the sky, that I tasted the deepest of my joy.

Early on a summer morning we would start from the outskirts of our little Berkshire town. Unfamiliar shadow under the home gables and strange quiet in park and market-place, I remember no family, no incident of departure, only the sense of known things passing away, and then, it seemed at once, the being roused from sleep in the midst of the fearful adventure of Paddington. I knew not then that Paddington was the aristocrat of the London termini with proud traditions and a leisurely staff. To me it was inferno; chaos with but one refuge, perhaps undiscoverable, the seaside train. The regulation Paddington train with its well-hung coaches panelled in ivory and brown, rolling smoothly westwards at the bidding of a decorously low-voiced bell-toned whistle, was, I thought, a vehicle kept in state for its glorious mission. Paddington has changed but little. The many buffets, the automatic machines and other modernities crowding the platforms accommodate themselves to its atmosphere. The staff, including the

smallest newspaper boy, is still courtly. And the turn
of the wheel that was bringing back mahogany and
repp has restored to the Great Western rolling stock
its Victorian garb of chocolate and cream to delight
the eye of survivors.

Paddington and piled luggage, and my family suddenly present. My mother, in sprigged muslin and
dustcloak and small round hat tilted nosewards from
piled hair, disquietingly anxious and dependent. My
sisters in sprigged cotton and reefers, their flushed
faces framed by monstrous 'zulu' hats, kept for the
seaside and most miserable in the wearing, with a
poke that hit the sky and was brought plastering
down over the ears by means of a tight bridle of elastic cutting, when new, unmercifully across beneath
the chin. A torment now banished for ever. It had
its compensations. You could, for instance, at
unobserved moments, by the simple device of working
the elastic to the tip of your chin, become a mounted
policeman – a painful process causing the coarse
straw to scrape the tender parts of your hot ears, and
dangerous unless you preserved a policemanlike
immobility. Usually you did not, and the elastic slid
and leapt, to come, with a cutting sting, tightly to rest
under your nose.

My father on these occasions was less tranquil
than the terminus, though quite as stately. Circumstances were exacting. All of us, including my mother
and the servants, reduced to eager and not always
mute helplessness, were pendant upon his omniscience, excited, frightened, and, but for him, lost
utterly. His to carry us through not only without help,
but hampered by the humiliating necessity of parting

with some of the finer shades of the composure inseparable from the bearing of the travelling English gentleman. This bearing was his by nature and by the grace of an almost religious cultivation. But the travelling English gentleman of his day clothed his composure in frieze and deerstalker, and though on these holiday flittings high summer seems always to have blazed, my father, whenever exposed to the vulgar gaze, bore these articles upon his tall and slender form. The long frieze, it is true, hung open, revealing the cool silky alpaca that lay beneath. But the weather and the occasion tyrannised. Useless to deny it – the English gentleman was flustered. Small wonder that my mother, goddess omnipotent, became almost one of ourselves, shared our torment: the certainty that the train would elude us. Small wonder, indeed, that my father shepherded the forlorn group into a waiting-room and forbade the opening of its door until he should reappear. To this day the inside of a waiting room recalls to me that fearful interval. Its terrifying length, the pictures of disaster that filled the small space so closely surrounded by large suggestive sounds. And its end was not the least of its fearfulness. The door would open quickly, not upon a stranger or a porter, but upon the dreaded form of my father, upon his voice, urgent. It was now or never. And the pilgrimage that ended in the security of our reserved carriage was made always in the certainty that this time it was to be never, that we alone amongst the small throng of travellers were doomed by some miracle to miss our heaven.

Once we were safely in the charm descended. Joy was secure. My mother, tearful with relief, would take up her twofold task of sympathy with our happiness and the protection of my father from disturbance. There was, however, an interval of licence lasting from the moment he stood up to free himself from his outer garments until he was ensconced, having for a while unbent to share our celebrations, sideways in his corner with his *Times*.

But the act of keeping comparatively still brought its own rewards. One could hear the faithful rumbling of the wheels, set now to hymn tunes sung quickly, and now, while the train sped rocking, and the telegraph wires, running together, refused to be counted, to a song of its own, the wordless, exultant beating, it seemed, of life itself. And the great events of the day came in the silence to life between memory and anticipation, blossomed in pictures upon the air vibrating to the song of the train. And suddenly there would be Basingstoke. Just a name, standing for a moment on its board on a platform and presently gone. Always for me it was the remotest point of our journey through unknown worlds, and always it filled me with a longing to escape the life I knew. I would look at the faces about me averted towards the platform, and wonder if they too knew where we were – on the borderland of what strange enchantment . . . After we had passed I suffered loss, as if something of me, alighting there, had been caught up into a state of being that knew no more of seaside and of home.

Quite different was faraway Exeter, 'Xturr, Xturr,' the porters would say conversationally. In high, fresh air. The first breath of the air that stood above the little seaside town. And these porters, because they breathed it, were different from other porters.

Belonging to the world of seaside, they looked happy
and serene, as if, though always there, they knew
quite well where they were. But these happy porters
stood in the distance at the end of the long day. The
sound of the wheels would begin to tell of the long,
long hours, and presently, unawares, I was wakening
from deep sleep to see the brown hamper open for
lunch, to feel older by a long day past, and blissful,
waking up after a party, to find another party just
begun.

By the time far Exeter was reached we children
were knowingly weary. And Exeter, with its message
of the sea's nearness, was trial – the last trial of the
day; a repetition in miniature of the agonies of Paddington. Like Paddington it was large, and, though
comparatively mild and gentle, still important and
awe-inspiring. To my childish imagination it was
purely in a spirit of respect for its manner and its size
that the train waited so long there. It was at Exeter,
too, that the sternest of my grandmothers joined us.
She was to the smaller of us little more than an appa-
rition. Once at the seaside she disappeared, doubt-
less preferring the quiet of independent lodgings to
the turmoil of our enchanted house. I cannot remember that she took any part in our life by the shore.
Only from time to time came the reminder that somewhere in the bright scene Grannie was abiding. It
was the only solemn thought that touched me during
the length of our stay. And the conviction – arising in
my mind if for long enough I stood staring at the
cascading waters beyond our door – that I was, in
the opinion of everyone but this laughing stream, a
very naughty girl – was cheerful compared to any

reflection on Grannie's sojourning. The first
intimation of her coming was the departure of my
father into the unknown. Once more we were left to
anxious helplessness, to the certainty of disaster.
Relief would come at last with the sound of Grannie's
voice – the high, staccato, wavering voice of
deafness and old age, crazing my childish nerves with
the imagined horror of a soundless world, chilling me
with the fear that the train, having stood so long,
would move on while she was being got in. There she
would stand, black-robed and towering between her
black-robed maid and one of ours, my father behind,
and my mother, all anxious helpfulness, inside the
carriage door.

But when at last she was arranged within there
was compensation for this large, dark presence with
its terribly chanting voice. When the speechless
greetings were over and my parents had communi-
cated with her by means of repeated shoutings into
the mouthpiece of the long tube hanging, a sinuous
black garland, across the carriage, she would, before
finally folding her hands to sit with eyes contempla-
tive upon each of us in turn, extract and distribute –
acid drops. The real lemon drops, that vanished with
the application of modern chemistry to lollipops. They
were strong. They contained the pure juice of the
lemon and the cane, were satisfyingly sweet and
acidly refreshing. They were also a noble size, square
and thick and with deep bevelled edges. They lasted.
But they were slippery. And if, their first charm
exhausted, the return of weariness brought a sudden
collapse, they slipped and lodged, four-square, half-
way down, and the end of the journey was sharp

pangs, pangs lessening and ending at last in forgetfulness, till lifting arms were there, and the window
and the sea where the train tunnels its way in and out
of the red cliffs along its edge. A strange, forbidding
sea, ghostly in fading light, as in the morning things
that been ghostly. An eternity, a child's whole day
with unfamiliar lateness added, had gone to the
making of a journey that now takes a few hours. But
the days to come were perhaps the richer for the joys
and agonies of that tremendous preliminary.

DATA FOR A SPANISH PUBLISHER

MY birth, towards the end of last century (in May 1873), bringing my parents their third daughter, was a disappointment to both of them, and my father, perhaps because I proved wilful, and sometimes quite unmanageable, early acquired the habit of calling me his son. Finally there were four daughters spending their very happy childhood in a spacious, large-gardened house near one of the loveliest reaches of the Thames and not far from the ancient university town of Oxford, whence elderly sages, visiting my father, would occasionally appear in our midst. Inheriting the whole of my grandfather's considerable business, my father had sold it and settled down to a life of leisure as an amateur of most of the arts and a deeply interested spectator of the doings of science, never missing a gathering, at home or abroad, of the British Association for the Advancement of Science, of which he was a member. Although his epicureanism, since his forebears for generations had been stern Puritans, was both fastidious and firmly disciplined, the spectacle of his existence nevertheless defined life to my dawning intelligence as perpetual leisure spent in enchanting appreciations.

My mother's life, too, was leisurely. Her ample staff of devoted old-fashioned servants loved and never left her unless it were to depart into marriage. She came of a long line of west country yeoman land-holders and although for the greater part of her life a semi-invalid it was she, our saint, who tried to make me see life as jollity, and, unconsciously, fostered my deep-rooted suspicion of 'facts' and ordered knowl-edge. From the first I hated, and whenever possible evaded, orderly instruction in regard to the world about me. Not that I lacked the child's faculty of wonder. In a sense, I had it to excess. For what astonished, and still astonishes, me more than any-thing else was the existence, anywhere, of anything at all. But since things there were, I preferred to become one with them, in the child's way of direct apprehension which no subsequent 'knowledge' can either rival or destroy, rather than to stand back and be told, in regard to any of the objects of my self-losing adoration, this and that. These objects were chiefly the garden, as known to me when no one was about, the woods, the sky, and sunlight.

'Education', therefore, came to me at first in the guise of a destroyer whom secretly I defied. At the age of five I attended for a year a small private school and willingly learned to read, fascinated by the vari-ety of combinations of letters and fired by the challenging irregularities of our unphonetic English spelling. All else went in at one ear and out at the other. When I was six, things began to move, and I recall, as if it were yesterday, the day when my life seemed to come to an end. We left our home. For two years, on account of my mother's health, we lived on the south coast in a hired house with alien furniture. The local school made no impression beyond increasing my ability to read and write. But the sea was there, though only the Channel sea in place of the boundless Atlantic of our summer holidays. It was there, day and night. From this unhomely home where, on an unforgettable night, I woke from a dream sobbing with the realisation that one day my parents would die, and feeling suddenly very old, we moved to the edge of one of the most charming of London's south-western suburbs, to a home that became for me, from the moment we turned in, from a wide roadway lined with pollarded limes, and drove up the approach between maytrees in bloom and swept round past a lawn surrounded by every kind of flowering shrub, to pull up in front of the deep porch of a friendly-faced, many-windowed house, a continuous enchantment: save when, by some apparently unprovoked outburst of wrath and resentment, I had scared and alienated all my family.

Until my eighteenth year, apart from intermittent distresses, over my mother's fluctuating health, and early secret worries produced by the problem of free will and the apparent irrationality of the Christian faith, life was very good and the future lay ahead bathed in gold. Music returned which from our seaside house had been almost absent. To the classics of my childhood were added the alien wonders of Wagner and Chopin, who alone among the moderns were fully welcomed by my father. The scores of Gilbert and Sullivan and other musical comedies,

eagerly purchased by my elder sisters after visits to
the theatre, also dance music and popular songs,
were relegated to the schoolroom piano, though the
usual sentimental ballads, and light instrumental
music, were welcomed at the 'musical evenings'
sandwiched between select gatherings of adepts for
classical chamber music. My sisters were growing up
and croquet on the front lawn was abandoned for
very strict tennis on the sunken lawn in the back
garden. Boating began, on the river near by. Skating in
the winter and, all the year round, dances increasingly
took the place of musical evenings. All this was to go
on for ever. For just one year after our arrival, life
was dimmed each day by the presence of a governess,
a worthy being who, if she could, would have formed
us to the almost outmoded pattern of female education: the minimum of knowledge and a smattering of
various 'accomplishments'. For me, apart from music
lessons and learning to join, without decorating them
with rows of blood dots, fascinatingly various scraps
of coloured material, she was torment unmitigated
and even her attempts at bribery, by gifts of chocolate mice, could not prevent my sliding, whenever
opportunity offered, under the table.

But school, when it came, was revelation. The
Head, a disciple of Ruskin, fostered our sense of fair
play, encouraged us to take broad views, hear all
sides and think for ourselves. We learned all about
our country's internal struggle against every sort of
absolutism. Some of us felt ourselves hoary sages
with a definite mission in life. Then there was Literature, and again the sense of coming into a goodly
heritage. Our aged literature master had been in his

youth a friend of Robert Browning and while inevitably he made us Browningites, he gave us through this one doorway the key to much else. In contrast to our Shakespearian teacher who insisted on our imbibing, with every few lines of a play, so many learned annotations that the very name of our great poet became a burden. Even so, there was still the fascination of words, of their sturdy roots, their growth and transformation, and the strange drama of the pouring in from every quarter of the globe of alien words assimilated and modified to the rhythm of our own speech, enriching its poetry and making its spelling and its pronunciation the joy of those who love it and the despair of all others. French, some of us painlessly acquired through sheer adoration of the white-haired old man, a scholar, who discoursed at large, gently told us tales, read to us, or dictated, French prose, taking for granted that we had learned, each week, the allotted page of rules. German came to us in a series of scenes, with a hot-tempered Fräulein of Junker birth and convictions, sometimes reaching proportions of sound and fury sufficient to bring in the Head from her study next door with oil for the troubled waters. To my inability to endure the teaching of geography unrelated to anything else on earth, I owed my removal, at the request of my parents to whom in my misery I had frantically appealed, from any geography lessons whatsoever and was placed, in compensation, in a class for the study of logic and psychology, newly introduced into the sixth form curriculum. Twice a week, among these stately elders, I delightedly acquired the rules of formal logic, joyously chanted the mnemonic lines representing the syllogisms and felt, with the growth of power to detect faulty reasoning, something akin to the emotion later accompanying my acquisition of a latch-key. Psychology, however, with its confidence and its amazing claims, aroused, from the first, uneasy scepticism.

In due course I found myself in the sixth form and head of the school. Almost unawares, for life was opening out and school had many rivals. Yet leaving school, in spite of all that seemed to lie ahead, was tragedy. Once more, it seemed, the end of life. But worse was to follow. My father, through disastrous speculation, lost the greater part of his resources. We were poor. The future offered no hope of redemption. Some of the servants were dismissed, their places being taken by my sisters, engaged to be married and willing, therefore, to explore the unknown mysteries of domesticity. It dawned upon me that I must make my own living. Since in those days teaching was the only profession open to penniless gentlewomen, I accepted, because I liked the idea of going abroad, the first post offered by the London agency I secretly visited: that of English teacher in a school in Germany. In vain my horrified family fought against this outrageous enterprise and to Germany I went, returning at the end of six months convinced that many of the evils besetting the world originated in the enclosed particularist home and in the institutions preparing women for such homes. An impression strengthened by further teaching experience, in school and family respectively. My sisters meantime had married. We had lost my mother and our home was finally broken up. Thrown on my own resources, longing to escape from the world of women, I gladly accepted a post with connections of my family, a secretarial job, daily, offering me the freedom I so desired. Transferring myself to a Bloomsbury attic, I existed for years on the salary of one pound a week, usual in those days for women clerks, scarcely aware of my poverty and never giving a thought to all I had left behind. In its place stood London and what London can mean as a companion, I have tried to set down in *Pilgrimage*. There were of course summer holidays, spent with friends at home and abroad, and weekends with relatives and friends with whom I shared old associations. Delightful restorative times of ease and orderly living. Also as much as I liked of various and interesting social life in company with the friendly household of my employers. But from all these excursions I returned to my solitude with the sense of escaping from a charming imprisonment.

During these London years I explored the world lying outside the enclosures of social life, and found it to be a kind of archipelago. Making contact with the various islands, with writers, with all the religious groups (from Roman Catholic to Unitarian and Quaker), with the political groups (from the Conservative Primrose League to the Independent Labour Party and Russian anarchists) and, through the medium of books and lectures, with the worlds of Science and Philosophy, I found all these islands to be the habitations of fascinating secret societies, to each of which in turn I wished to belong and yet was held back, returning to solitude and to nowhere, where alone I could be everywhere at once, hearing all the voices in chorus. The clear rather dictatorial

voice of Science-still-in-its-heyday, still far from con-
fessing its inability to plumb, unaided, the nature of
reality. Then the philosophers whom, reading, I found
more deeply exciting than the novelists. And the poli-
ticians, roaring irreconcilably one against the other,
unanimous only in their determination to exclude, by
almost any means, the collaboration of women from
the national housekeeping. The clerics, of all
varieties, still for the most part identifying religion
with morality and inevitably revealing, though with
naïve unconsciousness, in the definition of God presented to their congregations, the result of being
enclosed academies of males. For their God demanded
first and foremost docility, fear, blind obedience
and a constant meed of praise and adulation – all
typically masculine demands. The mystics, so far, I
had not encountered. Of art, apart from current
academic work, I knew next to nothing.

Experiments in being engaged to be married were
not entirely satisfactory. To be in love was indeed
fatally easy, and a condition I cannot recall escaping,
save for brief intervals, from adolescence onwards.
But to face up to marriage was another matter, and
on more than one occasion I withdrew a provisional
pledge. Sometimes the situation was reversed, my
partner being the one to retreat. For a moment the
Suffrage Movement diverted me from all else. Now
and again all seemed darkness within and without,
but always I failed to achieve, try as I would, a complete despair. At times the world-wide Catholic
Church seemed seductively to offer a refuge. But it
offered also the spectacle of the corrupting influence
of power. It needed the Protestants. Tragedy. Well, if

life were tragedy, it still was life, the ultimate astonisher.

Meanwhile I had begun to write. Translations and freelance journalism had promised release from routine work that could not engage the essential forces of my being. The small writing-table in my attic became the centre of my life. In 1907 I escaped into the country. A series of sketches contributed to the *Saturday Review* moved a reviewer to urge me to try my hand at a novel. A suggestion that both shocked and puzzled me. The material that moved me to write would not fit the framework of any novel I had experienced. I believed myself to be, even when most enchanted, intolerant of the romantic and the realist novel alike. Each, so it seemed to me, left out certain essentials and dramatised life misleadingly. Horizontally. Assembling their characters, the novelists developed situations, devised events, climax and conclusion. I could not accept their finalities. Always, for charm or repulsion, for good or ill, one was aware of the author and applauding, or deploring, his manipulations. This, when the drama was a conducted tour with the author deliberately present telling his tale. Still more so when he imagined, as did Flaubert, that in confining himself to 'Constatation' he remained imperceptible. In either case, what one was assured were the essentials seemed to me secondary to something I could not then define, and the curtain-dropping finalities entirely false to experience.

The first chapter-volume of *Pilgrimage*, begun in 1913, was finished just before the outbreak of war. Various publishers refused it and it finally appeared in the autumn of 1915. Meanwhile I had met my husband, an artist, who introduced me to a new world, the missing link between those already explored. In 1917 we were married, risking the adventure in spite of misgivings on both sides. These have been falsified and we are still married.

August 1943

Col

Virago Modern Classics

Dorothy Richardson

Journey to Paradise

'There is no one word, such as romance or realism, to cover, even roughly the works of Miss Dorothy Richardson . . . She has invented a sentence we might call the psychological sentence of the feminine gender' – *Virginia Woolf*

'She was writing of an actual struggle when the world for women was a prison, not a universe' – *Bryher*

Published together for the first time are Dorothy Richardson's short stories: delicate and slippery tales which range from the vast gardens of childhood and the anticipation of seaside holidays, to the shifts in perception as youth stutters towards maturity and on to the levelling experiences of old age and death. Accompanying this range of fictional voices are her autobiographical sketches, offering insight into Dorothy Richardson's life and the development of her creative talent.

With the publication of *Pilgrimage*, and her innovatory use of what came to be called the 'stream of consciousness' technique, Dorothy Richardson was hailed as the greatest woman genius of her time. That novel was her vocation, but it was not the sole achievement of her career. Embracing material which originally appeared in periodicals between 1919 and 1959, and including two previously unpublished stories, this volume reveals the extent of her creative agility. *Journey to Paradise* is a valuable addition to twentieth-century literature.

The cover shows
'A Corner of the Artist's Room in Paris'
by Gwen John.
Reproduced by kind permission of
Sheffield City Art Galleries.

£5.99 net in UK only

Fiction

ISBN 1-85381-050-9

9 781853 810503

G 9L